the earl's impossible bargain

AN ENEMIES TO LOVERS REGENCY ROMANCE

SHAYE MUIR

The Earl's Impossible Bargain
Copyright © 2025 by Shaye Muir
All rights reserved.

Book Cover and formatting provided by Trisha Fuentes
https://bit.ly/m/trishafuentes

No part of this book may be reproduced in any form or by any electronic or mechanical means, including information storage and retrieval systems, without written permission from the author, except for the use of brief quotations in a book review.

ISBN: 979-8-3485-6170-3 (Paperback)

**Published by
Ardent Artist Books**
www.ardentartistbooks.com

about ardent artist books

➥ ABOUT US

Ardent Artist Books was established in 2008

We publish modern and historical romances once a month!

Get Your FREE List: Published & Upcoming Books
visit our website at:
https://bit.ly/3Wva4o0

* * *

➥ WE HAVE BOOK TRAILERS

Follow us on YouTube!

https://bit.ly/3W3xn7a

Like, Subscribe & Comment

* * *

 WE HAVE SERIALIZED FICTION!

Visit our website today to download one of our stories that unfold in bite-sized pieces!

Each installment is just 99¢!

https://bit.ly/3LsDpJL

contents

1. An Unwanted Arrangement — 1
2. The Morning's Work — 15
3. First Impressions — 29
4. The Grand Entrance — 43
5. A Noble's Duty — 55
6. Thunder and Lightning — 69
7. She is Mine — 79
8. Rain on My Window — 95
9. A Quiet Dinner Party — 107
10. The Pianoforte — 121
11. Passion Erupts — 133
12. Proclaimed Intention — 147
13. A Spectacle of Myself — 161
14. Hyde Park — 171
    Epilogue — 183

YOU MIGHT ALSO LIKE
Marquess Made for Me — 197
Love in Winter — 199
Love Without Warning — 201

About Shaye — 203
Also by Shaye — 205

CHAPTER ONE
an unwanted arrangement
LADY ISABEL AINSWORTH

The morning sun streams through the tall windows of our morning room, casting golden ribbons across the pianoforte keys beneath my fingers. I lose myself in Beethoven's Sonata No. 14, letting the haunting melody sweep away my thoughts. The piece has always spoken to my soul - its delicate balance of light and shadow, of passion and restraint.

My fingers dance across the keys, finding each note with practiced precision. This is my sanctuary, these precious morning hours when the house is still quiet and I can simply be myself, unfettered by the endless social obligations that come with being the Earl of Ainsworth's daughter.

The melody flows through me like water over smooth stones, each note a memory. Mother taught me to play when I was barely tall enough to reach the keys, perching me on her lap as her gentle hands guided mine. Those memories are hazy now, soft-edged like a watercolor painting left in the sun, but the music remains crystal clear.

I shift into a more challenging passage, my fingers flying across the ivory. "You must feel the music in your soul, my darling," she would say. "Let it speak through you." Those were among her last words to me before the fever took her, leaving me at four years old with only the piano to remember her by.

Father tried his best after she died, though his idea of raising a daughter consisted mainly of hiring a parade of governesses and music instructors. I cannot fault him entirely - many young ladies of my station barely see their parents at all, relegated to nurseries and schoolrooms until they are old enough to be presented to society. At least Father takes breakfast with me each morning, even if our conversations rarely venture beyond weather and social obligations.

My hands falter slightly on the keys as I recall overhearing the butler and housekeeper discussing Father's latest losses at White's. They didn't know I was in the library alcove, hidden behind the heavy curtains with my novel. "Three thousand pounds," Mrs. Hopkins had whispered, her voice heavy with concern. "And that's just what we know of."

I press harder into the keys, letting the crescendo drown out the worry that constantly gnaws at my conscience. *We are fortunate,* I know this. Ainsworth Hall has been in the family for generations, its grounds stretching across some of Yorkshire's finest countryside. But estates require money to maintain, and Father's weakness for cards and dice threatens to drain what remains of our resources.

The music shifts again, my fingers finding their way through the complex harmonies that had taken months to master. I remember my first real piano instructor, a dour German woman who rapped my knuckles with a ruler when I missed a note. But even her harsh methods couldn't diminish my love for music. If anything, her strictness pushed me to excel, to prove I could master any piece she put before me.

"A lady must have accomplishments," Father always says, as though my dedication to music is merely another box to tick off on the list of marriageable qualities. He doesn't understand that when I play, I'm not performing for some future husband's drawing room. I'm speaking the language of my heart, the only way I know how to express the depths of feeling that propriety demands I keep hidden.

The morning light grows stronger, warming my shoulders through my muslin dress. Soon the household will be fully awake, and I'll need to attend to my duties as the lady of the house. There will be menus to approve, calling cards to answer, and all the thousand little tasks that keep our social position secure. But for now, I lose myself in the final movement of the sonata.

My mother's portrait hangs above the pianoforte, her brown eyes - so like my own - seeming to watch over me as I play. Sometimes I imagine I can see her smile when I master a particularly difficult passage, though the artist captured her in one of her more serious moments. She looks so young in the painting, barely older than I am now.

"You are so like her," Father sometimes says, usually after too much port in the evening. Those are the rare moments when his guard drops, when the weight of responsibility and worry falls away, and I glimpse the man my mother must have loved. But such moments never last long before he remembers himself, straightening his cravat and clearing his throat before returning to his usual topics of weather and social obligations.

CHAPTER ONE

The final notes of the sonata hang in the air like morning mist, slowly fading into silence. I keep my hands on the keys, reluctant to break the spell of these private moments. Soon enough, the real world will intrude with all its demands and expectations. Soon enough, I will need to be Lady Isabel Ainsworth, daughter of the Earl, mistress of Ainsworth Hall, everything proper and correct.

But for now, I am simply Isabel, my mother's daughter, letting my heart speak through the music she taught me to love.

A discordant note breaks my concentration as the morning room door creaks open. I pause, my hands hovering above the keys as Margaret, my lady's maid and dearest friend, hurries in. Her face bears an expression I've rarely seen - concern mixed with something that makes my stomach tighten.

"My lady, I apologize for the interruption, but your father requests your immediate presence in his study."

I press my fingers to the cool ivory keys, not yet playing. "Now? He knows this is my practice time."

"He was most insistent, my lady."

The knot in my stomach grows tighter. Father has never interrupted my morning practice - not since Mother died and I took over her beloved pianoforte. He knows how sacred these hours are to me.

"Did he say why?"

Margaret shakes her head, her brown curls bouncing slightly. "No, my lady. But he's been pacing. And fidgeting with his ring."

My father only fidgets with his signet ring when something truly troubles him. I rise from the bench, smoothing my morning dress. "Very well."

The walk to Father's study feels longer than usual, each step echoing against the polished floors. When I enter, the familiar scent of leather-bound books and brandy fills my nose, but something is different. Father stands by the window, his back to me, hands clasped behind him. He's wearing his best morning coat - the one reserved for important meetings.

Father had always been the handsomest man in any room, even now as worry lines crease his distinguished features. The morning light streaming through his study windows catches the silver threading through his reddish-brown hair - the same shade as my own. How many times have I heard whispers at balls and dinner

CHAPTER ONE

parties? "Lady Isabel is the very image of Lord Ainsworth in his youth." The comparison never fails to warm my heart.

I study his profile as he continues to gaze out the window, noting how his shoulders remain straight despite whatever burden weighs upon him. Even in moments of distress, he carries himself with the bearing of his station. The same pride that sometimes frustrates me also commands my deepest admiration.

"You wished to see me, Father?" I keep my voice steady, though my fingers still tingle with the remnants of Beethoven's melody.

He turns, and for a moment I catch a flash of something in his expression - regret? Fear? But it vanishes behind his usual mask of paternal authority. "Isabel, my dear. Yes. Please, sit down."

He begins to pace, his fingers finding their way to his signet ring. Three turns clockwise, then two counterclockwise - his tell when wrestling with difficult decisions. I've watched him do this countless times, usually before announcing some new economy measure or refusing an invitation we can no longer afford to accept.

"I've always tried to do what's best for you, Isabel.

Everything I've done - every decision I've made - has been with your future in mind."

The knot in my stomach tightens further. This preamble, so unlike his usual direct manner, can herald nothing good. I sit straighter, channeling the poise my governesses drilled into me through countless lessons.

"Of course, Father. I've never doubted that."

He pauses his pacing to look at me, and I see the same strong jaw, the same proud bearing that I've inherited. Even his way of lifting his chin slightly when gathering courage - I catch myself doing the same thing in difficult moments.

"You are nineteen now. A woman grown. It's time we discussed your future in earnest."

My fingers curl into my skirts, but I keep my expression neutral. "My future?"

"Yes." He resumes his pacing, the morning light catching the silver in his hair with each turn. "You've had your Season in London. While you acquitted yourself admirably in terms of deportment, you've shown... reluctance... in terms of securing an advantageous match."

CHAPTER ONE

I open my mouth to protest - surely one Season is not enough to determine one's entire future - but he raises a hand, so like my own in shape and gesture. The same long fingers meant for piano keys, though his have never touched ivory.

"No, let me finish. I understand your desire for romance. Your mother was the same way. But there are realities we must face, responsibilities that come with our position. The Ainsworth name carries weight, but names alone cannot secure a future."

The word "future" echoes in my mind like a discordant note. Future. Such a vast, nebulous concept that I've deliberately avoided contemplating. My thoughts rarely venture beyond planning tomorrow's menu or selecting which piece to practice on the pianoforte. Even during my Season in London, I focused on each ball, each musical performance, each social call as it came - never allowing myself to peer too far ahead into that intimidating void called "the future."

"Isabel?" Father's voice pulls me from my reverie. "Are you attending?"

"Yes, of course." I smooth my skirts, more for something to do with my hands than for any real need. "I simply... that is..." The words tangle on my tongue, unlike my usual facility with language. "I confess I don't quite understand your meaning, Father."

He sighs - that particular sigh I've heard more frequently of late, the one that speaks of burden and responsibility. His fingers work at his signet ring with increased vigor, and I notice his cravat is slightly askew, though he'd never permit such disarray were he receiving anyone else.

"Your mother and I..." He pauses, swallows hard. Even now, fifteen years after her death, speaking of her causes him visible pain. "We had an arrangement, you see. Before we ever met. Our families had agreed..."

My heart begins to pound against my ribs like the hammers striking piano strings. Surely he cannot mean... But the way he avoids my direct gaze, the formal coat, the nervous fidgeting - all pieces of a puzzle I desperately wish not to solve.

"Father?" My voice emerges higher than intended, closer to the child I was than the woman I've become. "What exactly are you trying to tell me?"

He finally stops pacing, placing both hands on his desk and leaning forward as if the mahogany might offer him strength. "The thing is, my dear, I've been in discussions. About your future. About securing the family's position."

CHAPTER ONE

The morning room suddenly feels too warm, too close. The sunlight that had seemed so golden and welcoming now feels harsh, exposing. I want to flee back to my pianoforte, to lose myself in Beethoven's familiar patterns rather than face whatever is coming.

"Discussions?" I manage to keep my voice level, though my fingers have knotted themselves in my skirts again. "With whom?"

"With the Earl of Brampton." Father straightens, apparently having found his resolve. "More specifically, about his heir, Lord William."

Lord William Brampton. The name strikes me like a physical blow. I've heard of him, of course - who hasn't? His reputation for cold efficiency in managing his father's estates is matched only by his apparent disdain for the marriage mart. Last Season, I'd glimpsed him at a few events, always standing apart, his golden hair and striking height making him impossible to miss. But we'd never been introduced, never exchanged so much as a word.

"I don't understand," I say, though the horrible truth is beginning to dawn. "What could Lord William Brampton possibly have to do with my future?"

Father's expression softens slightly, and for a moment I see the papa who used to lift me onto his shoulders, who would sneak me sweets before dinner. "My dearest girl, surely you must have known this day would come. You are of an age to marry, and Lord William is in need of a wife. The match would be most advantageous for both families."

The room spins slightly. Marriage. To Lord William Brampton. The man whose icy blue eyes I'd observed from across ballrooms, whose very presence seemed to lower the temperature of any gathering he attended. The man who, if rumors were to be believed, viewed marriage as nothing more than a business transaction to be negotiated and concluded with maximum efficiency.

"But..." I search for words, for arguments, for anything to halt this nightmare before it solidifies into reality. "But we've never even met! He doesn't know me, I don't know him. How could you possibly arrange such a thing?"

He stops pacing and faces me, his expression a mixture of determination and what looks suspiciously like guilt. "You are to marry Lord William. The banns will be read this Sunday."

The room spins slightly. "I beg your pardon?"

"It's a perfect match, my dear. The joining of two great families. The Brampton estates are extensive, and William has proven himself an excellent manager of—"

CHAPTER ONE

"Father." My voice comes out sharper than I intend. "You've arranged my marriage without consulting me?"

He sighs, shoulders sagging slightly. "Isabel, you must understand. Times are... difficult. The estate..." He trails off, running a hand through his graying hair. "Lord William is a fine young man. He'll make an excellent husband."

"An excellent husband?" I stand, my fingers curling into fists at my sides. "How would you know? Have you asked about his character? His temperament? Whether he has any interest in music or literature or anything beyond managing his precious estates?"

"Now, Isabel—"

"Does he even want to marry me? Or is he simply doing his duty like a good son?"

Father's expression hardens. "Sometimes duty must come before personal inclination. You are nineteen now. It's time you were settled."

"Settled?" The word tastes bitter on my tongue. "Like a piece of furniture?"

CHAPTER TWO
the morning's work
LORD WILLIAM BRAMPTON

I run my fingers along the precise columns of numbers in the estate ledger, feeling satisfied with the neat rows and balanced accounts. The morning sun streams through the study windows, illuminating the organized stacks of correspondence on my mahogany desk. Each pile represents a different aspect of the Brampton estate: tenant matters, investment opportunities, and social obligations.

A letter from our solicitor catches my eye, and I lift it to examine the seal. The morning's work stretches before me like a well-planned campaign, each task to be conquered in turn. This is where I excel, in the ordered management of our family's legacy.

The soft strains of a piano melody drift up from below - Mrs. Hornesbury at her morning practice. I pause in my calculations, allowing myself a moment to appreciate the familiar tune. She's played it since I was a boy, though never quite mastered the complex fingering in the third movement.

The familiar melody transports me back to Lady Sterling's ballroom three nights ago. Crystal chandeliers had cast their warm glow over the assembled ton, while delicate strains of Mozart floated through the air. I had stood near a marble column, observing the scene with carefully concealed weariness.

"Lord Brampton, you simply must meet my Prudence." Lady Beaumont had practically dragged her daughter forward, the girl's face flushed pink with either excitement or embarrassment. "She's just completed her first Season."

I had offered the expected bow. "Miss Beaumont."

The girl had barely managed a curtsy before her mother launched into an extensive catalog of her accomplishments. "Prudence plays the pianoforte beautifully. And her watercolors - why, her art master says he's never seen such talent!"

CHAPTER TWO

I had nodded at appropriate intervals while scanning the room for an escape route. The same tired parade of accomplishments trotted out like prized horses at market. After her came the Honorable Miss Whitmore, who apparently spoke four languages - none of them particularly well, judging by her mangled attempt at French pleasantries. Then Miss Catherine Blackwood, whose supposedly legendary wit consisted mainly of agreeing with everything I said.

"You must save me a dance, Lord Brampton." Lady Sterling's niece had batted her eyelashes so vigorously I feared she might strain something. "I've heard such wonderful things about your skill in the quadrille."

I touch the bridge of my nose, remembering the headache that had begun to form that evening. The entire Season has been an endless procession of young ladies, each more eager than the last to secure the attention of one of London's most eligible bachelors. Their mothers hover like hawks, armed with lists of accomplishments and not-so-subtle hints about impressive dowries.

Mrs. Hornesbury hits a wrong note below, and I wince. The jarring sound matches my mood as I recall Lady Jersey cornering me near the punch bowl.

"My dear William, you cannot remain unmarried forever." She had fixed me with that penetrating stare that made her such a formidable leader of the ton. "A man in your position has certain obligations."

"I am well aware of my duties, Lady Jersey." I had kept my tone carefully neutral, though my jaw had clenched.

"Then you must know it's time to choose a bride. The ton is beginning to wonder if you're too particular, or perhaps..." She had left the implication hanging delicately in the air.

I shuffle the papers on my desk with more force than necessary. The ton can wonder all they like. I refuse to make the same mistake as my father - trapped in a loveless marriage of convenience, both parties retreating to separate wings of the house within a year. I've watched too many of my peers enter such arrangements, seen the light fade from their eyes as passion gives way to polite indifference.

The music from below shifts to a lighter melody, but my thoughts remain heavy. That night, I had danced with no fewer than six eligible young ladies, each one perfectly proper, perfectly accomplished, and perfectly dull. Miss Hampton had simpered about the weather. Lady Margaret's conversation consisted entirely of relating the latest on-dits about people I had no interest in. Even the much-praised Miss Deveraux, supposedly a great beauty, had proved to be little more than a pretty face with the personality of a tea cozy.

I stand and move to the window, watching as a pair of gardeners trim the hedges with precise movements. At least they know their purpose, unlike the parade of debutantes whose only aim seems to be securing a wealthy husband. The sunlight catches the gold signet ring on my finger - the ring that marks me as the future Earl of Brampton, the ring that makes me such an irresistible prize to the marriage-minded mamas of the ton.

"A man in your position," Lady Jersey had said, as if that explained everything. And perhaps it does. The weight of centuries of tradition and responsibility rests on my shoulders, demanding an heir, demanding a suitable countess, demanding conformity to society's expectations.

My quill scratches across the paper as I make another notation. Father's health weighs heavily on my mind, though I push the thought aside. His increasing hints about marriage and securing the succession have become harder to ignore. But there are more pressing matters requiring my attention.

I reach for the next letter, this one bearing the direction of our steward at the northern estate. The paper is thick beneath my fingers, likely containing the quarterly reports I've been awaiting. Before I can break the seal, a knock interrupts my concentration.

"Enter." I don't bother looking up from my work.

"My lord." Hawkins, our butler, stands in the doorway with perfect posture. "His lordship requests your immediate presence in his study."

I suppress a sigh. "I'm rather occupied at present, Hawkins. Perhaps after—"

"He was most insistent, my lord."

The subtle emphasis tells me all I need to know. Father is in one of his moods. I set down my quill with precise movements, careful not to let my irritation show. "Very well."

As I rise, I catch my reflection in the window. My cravat has come slightly askew during my work. I adjust it with practiced fingers, noting the dark clouds gathering on the horizon. They are a fitting backdrop for what promises to be an unpleasant interview.

"James." I address the footman hovering near the door.

CHAPTER TWO

"See that these letters are sorted by date and region. I'll attend to them upon my return."

"Yes, my lord." The young man's eager response reminds me of myself at his age, desperate to prove my worth.

"And do try not to confuse Norfolk with Suffolk this time." I allow a slight warmth to enter my tone, softening the criticism.

The corridor to father's study seems longer than usual, each portrait of previous Brampton Earls watching my progress with painted judgment. *How many times have I made this walk? How many lectures on duty and responsibility have those walls witnessed?*

The heavy oak door looms before me, its brass handle polished to a shine by generations of anxious hands. I straighten my shoulders, adjust my coat, and prepare myself for whatever awaits within. A lifetime of training has taught me to maintain perfect composure, regardless of the circumstances.

Father's study remains unchanged since my childhood - the same massive desk, the same leather-bound books lining the walls, the same faint smell of tobacco and brandy. The room practically breathes tradition and obligation.

"William." Father looks up from his desk, his face grave. "Sit down."

I take the appointed chair, noting how the leather creaks in exactly the same spot it has for the past twenty years. "You wished to see me, sir?"

"Yes." He shuffles some papers, a rare sign of uncertainty. "I've received a letter from Ainsworth. We've come to an agreement that will benefit both our families considerably."

My stomach tightens, though I maintain my expression of polite interest. "Indeed?"

"It's time you married, William. The arrangements have been made. You'll wed Lady Isabel Ainsworth before the Season's end."

The words hit me like a physical blow, though I allow no outward reaction. Inside, something rebels against this casual disposal of my future, this neat arrangement of my life without my consultation or consent.

"I see." My voice remains steady, controlled. "And I presume I have no say in this matter?"

"No," he says quickly.

CHAPTER TWO

My fingers curl into fists at my sides, the familiar weight of expectation settling around my shoulders like a leaden cloak. "And what of Lady Isabel's thoughts on this arrangement?"

"Her feelings on the matter are irrelevant." Father's voice carries that imperious tone I've heard countless times before. "As are yours. The contracts will be drawn up within the fortnight."

"Irrelevant?" The word tastes bitter on my tongue. "Just as Mother's feelings were irrelevant when you arranged her life with the same cold precision?"

Father's face hardens. "You forget yourself."

"No, I remember perfectly well. I remember Mother retreating to the east wing while you buried yourself in this very study. I remember formal dinners where you barely exchanged two words. I remember—"

"Enough!" His fist crashes against the desk. "You will do your duty to this family, as I did mine."

"And look how splendidly that turned out." I rise from my chair, unable to contain my mounting fury. "Shall I follow your excellent example? Marry a stranger, produce an heir, then spend the next thirty years avoiding my wife's company?"

"You dare—"

"Yes, I dare. Because I've watched you live with your choices, Father. I've seen what a marriage of convenience does to people. And I refuse—" My voice rises despite my best efforts to maintain control. "I absolutely refuse to condemn myself and some innocent young woman to that same fate."

"You speak of things you don't understand." Father's voice has gone dangerously quiet. "This union will secure both families' futures. The Ainsworth estates border ours in Kent. Think of the advantages—"

"I don't give a damn about the advantages!" The words explode from me. "I won't be sold like a prized stallion to the highest bidder."

"You will do as you're told." Father rises, his height matching mine, though his shoulders have begun to stoop with age. "The arrangement is made. Your personal feelings are irrelevant."

"There's that word again. Irrelevant." I laugh, but there's no humor in it. "Tell me, Father, was there ever a moment in your marriage when you didn't regret choosing duty over love?"

CHAPTER TWO

The crack of his palm against my cheek echoes through the study. I don't flinch, though the skin burns.

"You will marry Lady Isabel." Each word falls like a hammer blow. "You will secure our family's future. And you will never speak to me of your mother again."

I touch my cheek, feeling the heat of the strike. "As you wish, my lord." I offer him a bow so precise it borders on insult. "After all, what are personal feelings compared to the mighty Brampton legacy?"

"William—"

But I'm already striding toward the door, my boots clicking against the polished floor. I pause with my hand on the handle. "I wonder, Father, if you'll ever realize that in trying to preserve our family's greatness, you've succeeded only in destroying its heart."

I exit before he can respond, slamming the door with enough force to rattle the family portraits in their gilt frames. Let them rattle. Let the stern-faced Brampton ancestors judge me from their lofty perches. I've spent my entire life trying to live up to their expectations, and where has it led?

To this. To being bartered away like a piece of property,

my future decided in an exchange of letters between two old men who've forgotten what it means to feel.

The irony of it all makes me want to laugh, or perhaps break something valuable. All those debutantes I've been avoiding, all those careful maneuvers to maintain my independence, and in the end, it makes no difference. I'm to be shackled to a woman I've never met, all in the name of duty and family obligation.

Lady Isabel Ainsworth. I've heard the name, of course. Everyone has. But beyond vague mentions of musical talent and a sharp tongue, I know nothing of the woman I'm expected to pledge my life to. Does she share my fury at this arrangement? Or is she, like so many of her peers, simply grateful to secure an advantageous match?

CHAPTER THREE
first impressions
LADY ISABEL AINSWORTH

The carriage jolts to a stop before the imposing facade of Brampton House, and I take a steadying breath. Through the window, I observe white stone columns rising against grey skies, the architecture as austere as I imagine its inhabitants to be. Father shifts beside me, his presence a reminder of why I am here.

"Remember your manners, Isabel," he murmurs, though we both know I am perfectly capable of proper etiquette when required.

I smooth my pale blue morning dress, chosen specifically to appear demure and unremarkable. "Of course, Father. I shall be the very picture of propriety."

He eyes me with suspicion, no doubt noting the glint in my eyes that I cannot quite suppress. The footman opens our carriage door, and I accept his hand with practiced grace.

The butler who greets us is as formal as the house itself, leading us through a marble-floored entrance hall that echoes with each step. Portraits of stern-faced Bramptons line the walls, their eyes following our progress. I lift my chin, refusing to be intimidated by mere paintings.

We are announced into a drawing room decorated in shades of blue and gold, where the Earl of Brampton rises from his seat. He is a thin man with sharp features and graying temples, but my attention is immediately drawn to the figure standing by the window.

Lord William Brampton turns, and I nearly falter in my steps. No one warned me he would be quite so handsome, and... tall. He towers over most men, I suspect, with broad shoulders that his perfectly tailored coat does little to disguise. Golden hair catches the weak morning light, and those eyes—piercing blue and entirely too observant—fix upon me with an intensity that makes my pulse quicken.

I drop into a curtsy. "Lord Brampton."

CHAPTER THREE

"Lady Isabel." His voice is deep, cultured, and carries not a hint of warmth. He bows with precise formality.

I force myself to maintain perfect posture as Lord William's gaze travels the length of my form, his blue eyes darkening ever so slightly. A peculiar tension fills the air between us, and I find myself holding my breath without meaning to. His jaw tightens, and something flickers across his expression—appreciation, perhaps?—before being swiftly masked by cool indifference.

"I trust your journey was pleasant?" He speaks with such precise control that it borders on mechanical.

"As pleasant as one might expect when being carted across London like a parcel to be delivered." The words slip out before I can stop them, earning me a sharp look from Father.

But I catch the briefest twitch at the corner of Lord William's mouth before he suppresses it. "Indeed. Though I dare say parcels rarely arrive in such..." His eyes sweep over me again, lingering a moment too long. "...fine packaging."

Heat creeps up my neck at his words, though whether from anger or something else entirely, I cannot say. The Earl of Brampton clears his throat, and we all turn to face him like chastened children.

"Shall we be seated?" The Earl gestures to the elegant arrangement of chairs and settees.

I choose a seat near the window, noting how Lord William's gaze follows my movement. He remains standing, one hand gripping the back of a chair with perhaps more force than necessary. The morning light catches his profile, highlighting the strong line of his jaw and the almost severe set of his mouth. Yet there's something in the way he holds himself—a certain tension—that suggests he's not quite as composed as he wishes to appear.

"Lady Isabel," he says, finally claiming his own seat. "I understand you're accomplished at the pianoforte."

"I play tolerably well." I smooth my skirts, watching his reaction. "Though I fear my selections tend toward the... passionate rather than the proper."

His eyes flash at that, and I see his fingers flex against his knee. "How fortunate then that propriety is not always the measure of true worth."

"Is it not?" I tilt my head, studying him. "I was under the impression that propriety was the very foundation of this... arrangement."

"Isabel," Father warns quietly.

But Lord William leans forward slightly, and I catch a glimpse of something almost predatory in his expression. "Arrangements, my lady, can accommodate many things beyond mere propriety. The question is whether one has the courage to explore them."

My breath catches at the challenge in his voice. We stare at each other for a long moment, and I realize with startling clarity that Lord William Brampton is far more dangerous than I'd anticipated. Not because of his position or his power, but because something about him makes me want to discover what lies beneath that carefully controlled exterior.

"I've always found courage to be a rather relative quality," I say, proud that my voice remains steady. "What seems brave to one might appear foolish to another."

He shifts in his chair, and I notice his knuckles have whitened where he grips the armrest. "And which would you prefer to be considered, Lady Isabel? Brave or foolish?"

"Neither, my lord. I would prefer to be considered honest."

His eyes darken further, and for a moment, I glimpse something raw and wanting in their depths before he masters himself. The air between us feels charged, like the moment before a storm breaks.

Our fathers exchange glances, but I barely notice. I'm too caught up in this strange battle of wills with a man who seems determined to match me word for word, challenge for challenge. It's thoroughly unsettling—and utterly thrilling.

Lord William rises suddenly, moving to pour himself a glass of water from a crystal decanter. I watch the controlled precision of his movements, sensing that each one is deliberately measured to maintain his composure. When he turns back, his face is once again an impassive mask, but I've seen enough to know what lies beneath it.

"Honesty," he says finally, "can be the most dangerous quality of all."

"Yes, honesty," I repeat, watching my father pause at the door.

"We shall leave you young people to become acquainted," the Earl of Brampton announces, exchanging a meaningful look with my father. "Mrs. Winters will chaperone, of course."

The elderly chaperone settles into a chair by the fire, her knitting already in hand. I take a seat on the blue damask sofa, arranging my skirts with deliberate care while Lord Brampton moves to stand before the fireplace, his shadow falling across my lap. "Honesty? Then let me be honest, my lady. I find this arrangement as appealing as a dose of laudanum."

"How fortunate we agree on something." I lean forward slightly, lowering my voice. "Though I must say, laudanum might be preferable to a lifetime of morning conversations such as this."

A strange light enters his eyes—something almost like amusement quickly masked. "You are not at all what I expected."

"No? Did you anticipate a simpering miss, eager to secure an advantageous match?"

"I expected someone less…" He pauses, searching for the word. "Direct."

A soft snore draws our attention to Mrs. Winters, whose chin has dropped to her chest, knitting needles still in her slack hands.

"How convenient," I murmur, rising to my feet. "Now we may speak plainly, my lord. I have no intention of marrying you."

He steps closer, his voice equally low. "Nor I—you, though our fathers seem determined to ignore our preferences."

"Then perhaps we should give them reason to reconsider."

His eyebrow lifts. "What exactly are you suggesting, Lady Isabel?"

"An alliance of sorts. Surely between the two of us, we can devise ways to demonstrate our complete unsuitability for one another."

I study Lord William's face as he processes my suggestion, fascinated by the subtle play of expressions across his features. A muscle ticks in his jaw, and those striking blue eyes narrow with consideration. He's devastatingly handsome when he's plotting something, I realize with an unwelcome flutter in my stomach.

"An alliance?" His voice drops even lower, sending an unexpected shiver down my spine. "Do elaborate, Lady Isabel."

"Well, my lord, since we both wish to avoid this marriage, we merely need to convince our fathers that we would make each other thoroughly miserable." I take a step closer, close enough to catch the faint scent of sandalwood and leather that clings to him. "Though I must say, your current demeanor of cold disapproval is an excellent start."

A flash of genuine amusement crosses his face, transforming his severe features into something altogether more dangerous. "Whereas your sharp tongue and apparent disdain for propriety are equally promising."

"I do try." I offer him my sweetest smile, the one that always makes Father nervous.

Lord William's lips twitch. "I begin to think you don't try at all."

The observation catches me off guard, as does the warmth in his tone. I find myself studying him more closely – the way his golden hair falls slightly forward when he tilts his head, the elegant strength of his hands as they grip the mantel, the surprising intelligence in those blue eyes that keep finding mine.

This is not at all what I expected. I had prepared myself for a stuffed shirt, a younger version of his father perhaps, all rigid propriety and cold duty. Instead, I discover a man who can match my wit and possibly even appreciate it. A man who seems to see beyond the carefully constructed facade of the perfect debutante.

How dreadfully inconvenient.

"You sound almost approving, my lord," I say, trying to maintain my composure. "That won't do at all if we're to convince our fathers this match is unsuitable."

He steps closer, and I become acutely aware of how he towers over me. "Perhaps I simply appreciate a worthy opponent."

"Opponent?" I arch an eyebrow. "I thought we were to be allies in this endeavor."

"Can we not be both?" His voice has taken on a rougher edge that does absolutely nothing to calm my racing pulse. "After all, the best partnerships often begin as rivalries."

I force myself to step back, needing distance from his overwhelming presence. "I believe you're missing the point, Lord William. We're not seeking any kind of partnership."

"Aren't we?" Those blue eyes fix on mine with unsettling intensity. "We're already plotting together, Lady Isabel. I'd say that's rather collaborative of us."

Blast the man for being clever. And charming. And possessed of a smile that transforms his entire face when he allows it to emerge. I had not counted on any of these

CHAPTER THREE

things when formulating my plans to avoid this marriage.

"You're enjoying this far too much," I accuse, though I can't quite keep the amusement from my own voice.

"Immensely." He doesn't even try to deny it. "Though I suspect you are as well."

He's right, curse him. What started as a desperate scheme to escape an unwanted marriage has somehow become an intriguing game with an equally intriguing partner. The way his eyes spark when we trade barbs, the subtle curve of his mouth when he's suppressing a smile, the sheer magnetism of his presence – all of it draws me in despite my best intentions.

"We should establish some ground rules," I say, more to distract myself from these troublesome observations than anything else.

"By all means." He gestures expansively. "Though I warn you, I've never been particularly good at following rules."

"How fortunate that I excel at breaking them."

This time he doesn't bother hiding his smile, and something warm unfurls in my chest at the sight of it. Oh, this is dangerous indeed. How am I to maintain my opposition to this marriage when every moment in his company makes me more curious about what lies beneath that carefully controlled exterior?

Mrs. Winters lets out another gentle snore, reminding me of our limited privacy. Lord William glances at her, then back to me, his expression turning serious.

"Shall we seal our pact then, Lady Isabel?" He extends his hand.

I regard it for a moment – his elegant fingers, the strength evident in his grip, the way my own hand might fit within it. Everything about this man seems designed to unsettle me, from his unexpected wit to his compelling presence.

"To our mutual unsuitability," I say, placing my hand in his.

His fingers close around mine, warm and sure, and I try desperately to ignore the jolt of awareness that shoots through me at the contact. This arrangement has indeed become interesting – perhaps *too* interesting for my peace of mind.

CHAPTER FOUR
the grand entrance
LADY ISABEL AINSWORTH

I sweep into the Huntington's ballroom with practiced grace, my emerald silk gown rustling with each step. The candlelight catches the gold embroidery at my hem, and I lift my chin, ready to execute our carefully crafted plan. But my composure falters the moment I spot him.

Lord William Brampton stands near the refreshment table, his golden hair catching the light from the chandeliers above. His commanding presence draws every eligible lady in the vicinity like moths to a flame. I watch as Lady Prudence Ashworth practically swoons when he offers her the barest hint of a smile.

My heart betrays me with a sudden flutter, and heat creeps up my neck. 'Tis merely nerves about our scheme, nothing more. I adjust my gloves, focusing on the delicate lace at my wrists rather than the way his evening clothes fit his broad shoulders so perfectly.

His gaze finds mine across the crowded room, and for a breathless moment, the air between us crackles with an energy I cannot name. Those piercing blue eyes hold mine, and I force myself to remember our purpose here tonight.

I turn away with deliberate slowness, as though his very presence offends me. From the corner of my eye, I notice several matrons watching our exchange with keen interest. Perfect.

"Lady Isabel." His deep voice carries across the space between us as he approaches for the obligatory dance. "I trust you are well this evening?"

"As well as one can be in present company," I reply, placing my hand in his with obvious reluctance.

The moment our fingers touch, awareness shoots through my arm like lightning. We take our positions for the quadrille, and despite our supposed animosity, our bodies move in perfect harmony. The dance brings us close, then apart, each turn executed with flawless precision.

"I see you've chosen to grace us with your presence tonight," he drawls as we circle each other. "Though perhaps grace is too generous a word."

"And I see you've chosen to favor us with your usual charm, my lord. Though charm might be too generous a word indeed." I match his tone precisely, even as I notice the subtle scent of sandalwood that clings to his coat.

"Your tongue remains as sharp as ever." His hand at my waist guides me through a turn, and I struggle to ignore how perfectly it fits there.

"Better sharp than dull, wouldn't you agree?" I counter, my skirts brushing against his legs as we move.

The dance continues, our barbed comments flying back and forth like well-aimed arrows, but underneath runs a current of something else entirely. When his fingers brush mine during a change of position, they linger a fraction too long. When we pass close enough that I can feel the heat radiating from his body, my breath catches traitorously in my throat.

"Lady Isabel," Lady Huntington's voice breaks through our dance-floor battle. "Would you honor us with a performance at the pianoforte?"

"Of course." I curtsey to William, noting how his eyes follow me as I make my way to the instrument.

I settle at the pianoforte, spreading my skirts carefully as I consider my selection. Lord Brampton positions himself where he can observe my performance, his stance critical and ready to find fault.

My fingers hover over the keys for a moment before I begin Nocturne in E-flat major. The passionate notes fill the room, and despite my intention to play poorly, my fingers refuse to cooperate. The music flows through me, expressing emotions I dare not name.

"Your tempo is uneven," William announces loudly as I finish. "And your interpretation lacks proper feeling. One might say it was almost mechanical."

The words sting more than they should, given our arrangement. I rise from the bench, my hands trembling slightly. "Perhaps, my lord, you might demonstrate your superior musical knowledge? Oh wait, you cannot play a note."

The assembled crowd gasps at our exchange, and I feel a flash of triumph even as something in his eyes makes my stomach flip. We've achieved our goal - everyone is watching our discord with rapt attention - but why does victory taste so bitter?

CHAPTER FOUR

Miss Marjorie Fairfax steps forward, her blue eyes flashing with indignation. "I found your performance quite moving, Lady Isabel. Perhaps you might favor us with Mozart's Sonata in C? I've heard you play it beautifully at the Pembrooke's musicale last month."

I hesitate, glancing at William's impassive face. His jaw tightens almost imperceptibly.

"Yes, do play again," Lady Huntington urges. "Lord Brampton's criticism seems rather harsh for someone who claims no musical talent himself."

I return to the pianoforte, my fingers finding their place on the keys. This time, I let the music flow naturally, each note pure and precise. The melody soars through the ballroom, and I lose myself in the complexity of Mozart's composition. For these precious moments, I forget our scheme, forget the watching crowd, forget everything but the music.

When the final notes fade, William's voice cuts through the appreciative applause. "Better technically, I suppose, though still lacking any real passion. One might say it was as cold as the performer herself."

I rise, my hands clenched at my sides. "How fascinating that you should lecture on passion, my lord, when you possess all the warmth of a marble statue."

Whispers ripple through the crowd. I catch fragments of conversation:

> *"Cannot believe they're to be married..."*
> *"Such obvious antipathy..."*
> *"Never seen two people more ill-suited..."*

The weight of their stares becomes unbearable. I flee to the garden, seeking refuge among the night-blooming jasmine. The cool air soothes my flushed cheeks as I grip the stone balustrade.

The night air fills my lungs as I struggle to slow my racing heart. My fingers still tingle from the keys, and I press them against the cool stone of the balustrade, seeking any measure of composure I can find. The jasmine's sweet perfume wraps around me, but even its familiar comfort cannot ease the tight knot in my chest.

Lacking any real passion. His words echo in my mind, sharp as thorns. They should not cut so deeply - *this is precisely what we planned, is it not? To show everyone how utterly incompatible we are?* Yet something in his tone, in the way his eyes had darkened when he delivered that calculated insult, leaves me unsettled.

I close my eyes, remembering how the music had flowed through me. Mozart - I had chosen it with such care—

had practiced it countless times until each note sang with perfect clarity. In truth, I had wanted him to hear the passion in every phrase, to recognize the depth of feeling I could express through my beloved instrument. *How foolish.* Even now, I cannot quite understand this sudden, desperate need to prove myself to him.

My hands clench against the stone as I recall his face during my performance. Though I kept my eyes fixed upon the keys, I had felt his gaze upon me, heavy and intense. Once, just once, I had glanced up to find him watching me with an expression I could not decipher - something raw and unguarded that vanished the moment our eyes met.

"Stupid, stupid girl," I whisper to the night air. "This is exactly what you wanted." But the words ring hollow, and I cannot ignore the way my heart had leaped when he entered the ballroom, how my skin had burned at his touch during our dance.

The music still echoes in my mind, but now it seems to mock me. Each perfect note a reminder of how desperately I had wanted to impress him, to show him that I was more than just the difficult, sharp-tongued woman I pretended to be. I had poured my soul into that performance, and he had dismissed it as cold and passionless.

Perhaps that is what stings the most - that in this moment of genuine feeling when I had let my guard down despite myself, he had chosen to wound me. *Or had he seen through my facade? Had he recognized the truth in my playing and deliberately struck where it would hurt most?*

I press my palm against my chest, willing my heartbeat to steady. The night breeze carries the sound of laughter and music from the ballroom, reminding me that I cannot hide here forever. Soon, I must return and continue our charade, must meet his cutting remarks with my own barbed wit. But for now, I allow myself this moment of honesty: I had played for him, only him, and his rejection - even a feigned one - has shaken me more than I care to admit.

Footsteps crunch on the gravel behind me. "Running away?" William's voice holds a dangerous edge.

I turn to face him. "Come to criticize my retreat as well? Perhaps my form was lacking?"

He moves closer, moonlight casting shadows across his features. "Your form is never lacking."

The words send heat coursing through my veins. "I thought you found me cold, my lord?"

"Perhaps I need to look closer." He steps nearer still, close enough that I can see the flecks of darker blue in his eyes. "To properly assess your... passion."

My breath catches. "You overstep, sir."

"Do I?" His fingers brush my arm, leaving trails of fire in their wake. "Or are you afraid I might discover you're not as immune to me as you pretend?"

I lift my chin. "The only thing I fear is dying of boredom in your company."

"Liar." He leans closer, his breath warm against my cheek. "Your pulse is racing."

And it is, treacherously so. The space between us crackles with tension. His gaze drops to my lips, and I sway forward unconsciously. We're close enough now that I can count his eyelashes, can feel the heat radiating from his body...

"Lady Isabel?" Lady Prudence's voice shatters the moment. "Your father is looking for you."

William steps back as though burned, and I struggle to compose myself. *What just happened? Were we still playing our roles, or was that something else entirely?*

I hurry past him, my skin still tingling where he touched me. As I rejoin the ball, one thought haunts me - I'm no longer certain if I'm pretending at all.

CHAPTER FIVE
a noble's duty
LORD WILLIAM BRAMPTON

I arrive precisely on time to Lady Worthington's garden party, as any proper gentleman should. The morning air carries a hint of approaching rain, though the sun still dominates the cloudless sky. Several of my fellow landowners have already gathered near the refreshment table, discussing the latest parliamentary actions affecting our estates.

I nod politely to Lady Worthington as she flutters past, directing servants with fresh flower arrangements. The gathering has drawn the usual suspects - lords and ladies seeking both pleasure and business opportunities under the guise of social niceties.

"Brampton! Just the man I hoped to see." Lord Fairfax approaches, his ruddy complexion suggesting he's already partaken generously of the port. "Have you heard about the canal project near Derbyshire?"

"I confess I have not." I accept a glass of lemonade from a passing footman, more to have something to occupy my hands than from any real thirst. "Though I imagine you're about to enlighten me."

"Indeed." Fairfax lowers his voice, glancing around conspiratorially. "Parliament has approved the new waterway. Construction begins this autumn. The route passes through several promising parcels of land - currently worthless fields, but soon to be prime commercial frontage."

I raise an eyebrow, my interest genuinely piqued despite Fairfax's theatrical delivery. "And you have inside knowledge of these parcels?"

"Better." He produces a folded document from his coat pocket. "I have options to purchase three of the most advantageous plots. The current owners have no idea of the canal's planned route."

"That seems rather..." I search for a diplomatic word, "opportunistic."

"Business, my dear fellow. Pure business." Fairfax unfolds the paper, revealing a carefully drawn map. "I'm offering you first chance at a quarter share. The initial investment is steep - five thousand pounds - but we stand to triple our money within two years."

I study the proposed route, noting how it connects to existing waterways. The potential is undeniable, yet something about the scheme leaves me uneasy. "The current landowners - are they local families?"

"Smallholders mostly. One widow with a failing dairy operation." Fairfax waves his hand dismissively. "They'll get fair market value for worthless grazing land. More than fair, really."

"And none have been informed of the canal project?"

"That information isn't public yet." He leans closer, breath heavy with port. "Which is precisely why we must act quickly. Others will catch wind of this soon enough."

I fold the map carefully, considering the proposition. The return would certainly help offset some of the estate's recent expenses, and the investment appears sound from a purely financial perspective. Yet I cannot shake the feeling that profiting from others' ignorance, however legal, falls short of true nobility.

"I'll need time to review the particulars," I say, returning the document. "Send the full proposal to my solicitor."

"Don't wait too long." Fairfax tucks the map away. "I have several other interested parties."

"Of course." I spot Lady Worthington approaching with a determined expression that suggests she means to introduce me to yet another eligible young lady. "If you'll excuse me, I believe our hostess requires my attention."

"Consider it carefully, Brampton." Fairfax calls after me as I make my strategic retreat toward the rose garden. "Opportunities like this don't come along often."

I weave through the crowd, acknowledging acquaintances with brief nods while maintaining enough momentum to avoid being drawn into conversation. The investment weighs on my mind. Five thousand pounds is not an insignificant sum, even for an estate as well-managed as Brampton. The potential return would provide a comfortable cushion against future uncertainties.

Yet I cannot help but think of that widow with her dairy farm. How many generations of her family worked that land, unaware that its true value lay not in honest labor but in its proximity to a line on some bureaucrat's map? The thought sits ill with me, like wine gone to vinegar.

A burst of familiar laughter draws my attention to a nearby gathering. Miss Korina Worthington stands among a group of young ladies, her green eyes bright with barely concealed mischief as she recounts some tale. Our gazes meet briefly before she turns away with studied indifference, though not before I catch the slight quirk of her lips that suggests she's enjoying our little flirtation.

"Brampton, what say you about the new grain tariffs?" Lord Fairfax gestures with his glass.

I launch into a detailed analysis of the economic implications, but my attention fractures at a flash of pale blue muslin through the crowd. Isabel. My throat tightens inexplicably - surely from irritation at her mere presence. She moves with natural grace through the gathering, her copper-touched hair catching the sunlight in a way that draws every eye. Including mine, much to my vexation.

I shift my position slightly, ensuring a clear view of her while maintaining my aloof demeanor. The pale blue of her gown complements her figure in a way that... I shake my head slightly. These observations serve no purpose beyond our mutual goal of appearing ill-matched.

"I say, Brampton, you've gone rather quiet," Lord Fairfax interrupts my thoughts.

"My apologies. I was considering the broader implications for the autumn harvest."

I excuse myself and move strategically through the crowd, positioning myself where I can best execute our plan. Yet my eyes keep returning to her of their own accord. The way she laughs at something Lady Pembroke says, the elegant turn of her wrist as she accepts a glass of lemonade. This awareness of her every movement is becoming most inconvenient.

When Isabel and several other young ladies make their way toward Lady Worthington's prized rose garden, I recognize the perfect opportunity to further our scheme. I wait a few measured moments before following, my mind already crafting appropriately cutting remarks about her surely limited knowledge of horticulture.

The rose garden's paths wind between carefully tended bushes, their blooms heavy with morning dew. Isabel moves ahead of her companions, reaching out to touch a particularly fine specimen of a pink rose. I round the corner, prepared to deliver my first barb, when she turns suddenly. Her hand brushes mine as she steps back in surprise.

The contact sends an unexpected jolt through my arm. Her scent - lavender and something uniquely her own - mingles with the roses' perfume. I find myself momentarily lost for words, my carefully prepared criticisms scattering like leaves in a breeze.

"Lord Brampton." Her voice carries just the right note of disdain. "How unfortunate to encounter you here."

I force myself to focus, to remember our purpose. "Lady Isabel. I see you're admiring the roses. Though perhaps you'd be better served studying proper deportment instead of botany."

"I assure you, Lord Brampton, my deportment is perfectly adequate. Unlike some who mistake cold arrogance for proper breeding." Isabel's eyes flash with challenge as she delivers the barb with precise aim.

I step closer, ensuring our exchange remains private despite its theatrical nature. "Better cold arrogance than overheated dramatics, my lady. Your performance at the pianoforte last week was particularly... passionate."

"Oh dear, are they at it again?" Lady Pembroke's carrying whisper reaches us clearly - intentionally, no doubt. "I cannot fathom why the Earl of Brampton would arrange such an obviously ill-suited match."

"Perhaps he hopes their mutual antipathy will spark into passion," her companion replies with equal volume. "Though I've never seen two people more determined to despise each other."

Isabel's lips twitch almost imperceptibly. We've drawn exactly the audience we intended. "At least I possess passion for something beyond ledgers and land management, my lord. Tell me, do you ever remove that stern expression, or has it become permanently fixed?"

"I reserve my smiles for those who merit them." I allow my gaze to drift pointedly past her shoulder. "Ah, Miss Worthington appears to be seeking company. If you'll excuse me, I shall endeavor to find more stimulating conversation."

"Lord Brampton!" Lady Worthington's voice cuts through the garden. She approaches with the determined air of a general leading troops into battle. "I simply must know what you and Lady Isabel find to quarrel about so consistently. One would think an engaged couple would show more harmony."

"I assure you, Lady Worthington," I reply smoothly, "Lady Isabel and I maintain perfect harmony in our mutual desire to maintain distance from one another."

"How can you speak so?" Lady Worthington fans herself vigorously. "Such discord between an affianced couple! It simply isn't done."

"Perhaps," Isabel interjects with sweet venom, "Lord Brampton might better spend his time studying social graces rather than criticizing mine. Though I fear even your excellent guidance would be wasted on such resistant material."

"Upon my word!" Lady Worthington's fan moves faster. "I have never... in all my years... Lord Fairfax, come speak sense to these young people!"

Lord Fairfax approaches port glass still in hand. "Lovers' quarrels should be conducted in private, wouldn't you say, Brampton? Though I must admit, your lady keeps you well matched in wit, if nothing else."

"Wit requires intelligence to appreciate it," Isabel remarks. "Perhaps that explains Lord Brampton's consistent failure to recognize mine."

The gathering crowd titters at her sharp reply. I fight back an inappropriate urge to smile at her quicksilver tongue. "Lady Isabel mistakes cutting remarks for wit. A common error among those who value quantity of words over quality."

"Better too many words than too few emotions," she counters. "Though I suppose one must possess feelings to express them."

"Children, children!" Lady Worthington interrupts. "This

display is most unseemly. Lord Brampton, surely you can find some common ground with your intended?"

I regard Isabel with carefully crafted disdain. "We share an equal desire to end this conversation, I believe. If you'll excuse me, Lady Worthington, I believe I see my father beckoning."

"Running away, my lord?" Isabel's voice carries the perfect note of challenge. "How characteristic."

"Not running, Lady Isabel. Merely seeking more profitable uses of my time." I bow slightly. "Though I'm certain you'll find someone else to practice your barbs upon. You do so enjoy an audience."

"Better an audience than a mirror, sir. At least I need not practice my disapproving expressions alone."

More whispers ripple through the growing crowd of spectators. I catch fragments of conversation:

> *"Never seen such obvious dislike."*
> *"What can their fathers be thinking."*
> *"Bound to end in disaster."*

Lady Worthington clutches her fan like a shield. "I simply cannot understand it. Two such eligible young people, from such excellent families... How can there be such discord?"

"Perhaps," Lord Fairfax offers, "it's merely high spirits. Young people today express affection so differently than in our day."

"If this is affection," Lady Worthington replies, "I should hate to see their true displeasure."

Isabel's eyes meet mine briefly, a flash of shared triumph in their depths. Our performance has achieved its desired effect. The ton buzzes with speculation about our obvious unsuitability. Surely our fathers cannot ignore such public discord indefinitely.

Yet something in her gaze unsettles me - a spark of something beyond our carefully orchestrated disdain. I find myself wondering what those eyes would look like warmed by genuine pleasure rather than calculated spite.

"Come, Isabel." Lady Pembroke steps forward to link arms with her friend. "Let us leave Lord Brampton to his important business. I'm sure he has ledgers pining for his attention."

"Indeed." Isabel allows herself to be led away, though not without a parting shot. "Do try not to strain yourself with excessive emotion, my lord. I know how it taxes you."

The approaching storm brings a freshening breeze, carrying the first drops of rain. The other guests begin to scatter, leaving us in an increasingly awkward position. Propriety demands I escort her to safety, yet she maintains our charade by stepping away from my offered arm.

"I require no assistance from you, my lord."

The rain intensifies suddenly, and without conscious thought, I gather her close and hurry her toward the waiting carriages. She feels impossibly right in my arms, her warmth seeping through the layers of clothing between us. When we reach her carriage, our eyes meet for a brief moment. The world narrows to just her face, raindrops clinging to her lashes, her lips slightly parted in surprise.

I force myself to step back, my control threatening to slip entirely. My hands tingle where they touched her, and I find myself adjusting my cravat, though it sits perfectly straight as always.

CHAPTER SIX
thunder and lightning
LADY ISABEL AINSWORTH

The rain pelts against the carriage windows with a fury that matches my inner turmoil. Lord Brampton sits across from me, his broad shoulders taking up far too much space in the confined interior. I press myself against the opposite wall, desperate to maintain what little distance remains between us.

His scent fills the small space—sandalwood and leather, mixed with something uniquely him that makes my head spin. I focus on smoothing my rain-dampened skirts, refusing to acknowledge how the wet fabric of his coat clings to his chest.

"Your assistance was unnecessary, my lord," I say, my voice coming out sharper than intended. "I am perfectly capable of entering a carriage on my own."

"Clearly." A drop of water falls from his golden hair onto his cheek. "Though your current state suggests otherwise."

With an elegant sweep of his hand, William pushes his rain-soaked hair back from his forehead. The simple gesture shouldn't affect me so, yet I find myself transfixed by the way his long fingers comb through the golden strands. A wayward droplet traces down his strong jaw, and I grip my hands tightly in my lap to keep from reaching out to brush it away.

My heart pounds against my ribs, and I know it has nothing to do with our dash through the rain. The close confines of the carriage make it impossible to ignore his presence—the way his knee occasionally brushes mine when we hit a rough patch of road, the subtle shifting of his powerful frame as he adjusts his position.

"You're staring, Lady Isabel." His voice holds that infuriating note of amusement. "Have I somehow offended your sensibilities by attempting to make myself presentable?"

I force my gaze to the window, though the streaming rivulets distort any view of the passing countryside. "I was merely noting how you manage to look as disheveled as ever, despite your best efforts."

The words lack their usual bite. My mind keeps returning to the moment I spotted him in Lady Worthington's garden, bent close to that insipid Miss Worthington as she simpered over her prized roses. The sight had sent an unexpected surge of... something through my chest. Certainly not jealousy—that would be preposterous. We are meant to be proving our incompatibility, after all.

Yet my fingers itch to smooth his cravat, which has come slightly askew in our mad dash to the carriage. I curl them more tightly into my skirts, fighting the traitorous impulse. The fabric of my gown is damp beneath my hands, and I focus on that discomfort rather than the warmth radiating from his body in the enclosed space.

"I must say," he drawls, "your performance today was particularly inspired. Though perhaps next time you might refrain from questioning my knowledge of crop rotation quite so loudly."

I chance another glance at him and immediately regret it. He's loosened his cravat slightly, and a glimpse of his throat makes my mouth go dry. "Your agricultural expertise hardly impressed Miss Worthington. She seemed far more interested in your... other qualities."

The words escape before I can stop them, and I want to sink into the carriage floor. William's eyebrows rise slightly, and I see that dangerous glint in his blue eyes—the one that always precedes some particularly cutting observation.

"I wasn't aware you paid such close attention to my interactions with other ladies." His voice drops lower, taking on a silken quality that sends shivers down my spine. "One might almost think you were—"

"Don't flatter yourself," I interrupt, though my voice sounds breathless even to my own ears. "I simply think it poor form to encourage her when we are meant to be..." I wave my hand vaguely between us, unable to find the right words with him looking at me so intently.

He leans forward slightly, and I catch another whiff of his scent—rain-dampened wool and leather, mixed with something spicy and masculine that makes my head spin. "When we are meant to be what, exactly?"

My hands practically burn with the need to reach out and touch him, to discover if his rain-chilled skin would warm beneath my fingers. I dig my nails into my palms instead, clinging to my rapidly fraying composure. "Proving ourselves an unsuitable match, of course. Or have you forgotten our arrangement already?"

"I assure you," he says softly, "I haven't forgotten anything."

CHAPTER SIX

The way he says it makes my breath catch, and I'm suddenly very aware of how small this carriage truly is. Another bump in the road sends me sliding forward on the seat, and his hand shoots out to steady me. Even through my gloves and sleeves, his touch burns like a brand.

"I find myself more intrigued by ladies who challenge me." His voice drops lower. "Those who hide fire behind proper manners and cutting words."

A crack of thunder splits the air. I jump, my hand flying to my chest—and somehow find myself mere inches from Lord Brampton. His breath fans across my cheek, and I realize I've grabbed his lapel.

"Afraid of a little storm, my lady?" His words are barely a whisper.

"No more than I fear you." But my voice trembles, betraying me.

His eyes drop to my lips. "Perhaps you should."

Another thunderclap booms overhead, but I barely hear it. All I can focus on is the way his hand has come to rest at my waist, the heat of it burning through my wet gown. My fingers are still twisted in his coat, and I should release him—I know I should—but I can't seem to make my hands obey.

"William," I breathe, not even realizing I've used his Christian name until it's already escaped.

He groans softly, and then his mouth is on mine. His lips are warm despite the chill air, and impossibly soft. One of his hands threads through my hair, cradling the back of my head as he deepens the kiss. I gasp against his mouth, and he takes advantage, his tongue sweeping inside to tangle with mine.

I should push him away. This is madness—everything we've worked toward, our careful plan to appear incompatible, all of it crumbling in the face of this overwhelming need. Instead, I find myself pulling him closer, my fingers sliding up to tangle in his damp hair.

He tastes of brandy and desire, and I drink him in like I'm dying of thirst. His thumb strokes along my jaw as he changes the angle, and I whimper at the increased pressure. Outside, the storm rages on, thunder rolling across the sky, but I barely notice. All I can focus on is the way his mouth moves against mine, the solid warmth of his chest under my palms, the slight scrape of stubble against my skin.

CHAPTER SIX

Without warning, William releases me, leaving me bereft and cold in the sudden absence of his warmth. My eyes burn with desire as I stare at him, my breath coming in short gasps that make my stays feel impossibly tight.

"Why?" The word escapes me in a broken whisper.

He shifts away, putting as much distance between us as the carriage allows. His hair has darkened from the rain, making his blue eyes appear even more striking—almost luminous in the storm-darkened interior. The sight of him, disheveled and breathing heavily, sends another wave of longing through me.

"I apologize, Lady Isabel." His voice is rough, sending shivers down my spine. "That was... unconscionable of me. I took advantage, and it shall not happen again."

Not happen again? My heart pounds so forcefully I'm certain he must hear it, must see how it threatens to burst from my chest with each beat. I want him to take advantage—again and again until I can't remember my own name. Until this maddening tension between us shatters completely.

"And if I wish it to happen again?" The words slip out before I can stop them.

William's eyes darken further, and his hands clench into fists on his thighs. A drop of rain slides down his throat, disappearing beneath his collar, and I follow its path with hungry eyes. How can he be even more handsome now, with his perfect composure in ruins? It isn't fair.

"You don't know what you're saying." He looks away, his jaw clenched. "This... attraction... it will pass. It must."

But I don't want it to pass. The realization hits me like a physical blow. I should be running in the opposite direction, putting as much distance between us as possible. This isn't part of our plan—this overwhelming need that makes my skin feel too tight, that makes me ache to close the distance between us again.

"William—" I reach for him, but he catches my hand before I can make contact.

"Don't." His thumb strokes once across my knuckles before he places my hand firmly back in my lap. "Please."

That single touch sends sparks racing up my arm. I curl my fingers into my skirts, trying to trap the sensation there. "You felt it too. I know you did."

"What I feel doesn't matter." His voice is clipped, controlled. "We agreed to end this arrangement. That hasn't changed."

But everything *has* changed. The air between us crackles with possibility, with wanting so intense it steals my breath. I should look away from the strong line of his jaw, the way his wet shirt clings to his shoulders. I should remember our carefully laid plans.

Instead, I memorize every detail of him in this moment —his usually perfect hair falling across his forehead, the slight swelling of his lips from our kiss, the way his chest rises and falls with each carefully measured breath. *When did he become so beautiful to me? When did his presence start feeling less like an irritation and more like a necessity?*

The carriage jolts to a stop, and reality crashes back in. We've arrived at my home, and in moments, we'll have to step back into our proper roles. The thought makes my chest ache.

"Isabel." He says my name like a prayer, like a warning. "This can't happen again."

But it already has. Everything has shifted, transformed into something new and terrifying and wonderful. As I step down from the carriage, my legs shaking beneath me, I know with bone-deep certainty that nothing will ever be the same.

CHAPTER SEVEN

she is mine

LORD WILLIAM BRAMPTON

I storm into Brampton Hall, barely acknowledging Winters, my butler, as he reaches for my dripping overcoat. My boots leave wet trails across the marble floor - something that would normally vex me to no end, but I cannot focus on such trivialities when my mind is consumed by what transpired in that carriage.

"Would you like a brandy brought to your chambers, my lord?" Winters asks, his voice carrying that knowing tone that makes me wonder just how much my face betrays.

"No. Have Thompson draw a bath." I take the stairs two at a time, needing the physical exertion to calm my racing thoughts.

In my chambers, I practically tear at my cravat, casting aside my rain-soaked garments with none of my usual care for proper order. The warm bath awaits, steam rising invitingly from the copper tub. I dismiss Thompson and sink into the water, hoping it might wash away the memory of her - but it only intensifies everything.

Isabel. The way she felt in my arms, the softness of her lips against mine, the small sound she made when I pulled her closer. It was meant to be pretense, this elaborate charade of ours. How utterly foolish we were to think we could maintain such artifice when every fiber of my being yearns for her presence.

The bathwater does nothing to cool the heat coursing through my veins. I close my eyes, but that only makes it worse - I see her there, those warm brown eyes darkened with desire, her copper-kissed hair coming loose from its pins, her chest rising and falling rapidly against the constraints of her corset.

My body responds traitorously to these thoughts, and I grip the edges of the tub, forcing myself to think of ledgers, crop rotations, anything but the way her fingers curled into my lapels or how perfectly she fit against me.

I splash cold water on my face, but the tension remains. I am a gentleman, I remind myself sternly. I will not dishonor her memory, even in the privacy of my own thoughts.

CHAPTER SEVEN

Standing abruptly, I reach for a towel, determined to regain my composure. But a treacherous voice whispers in my mind - if mere thoughts of Isabel can affect me so profoundly, what will it be like when she is truly mine? When there are no more pretenses between us?

I dress with mechanical precision, each button and fold a deliberate distraction. But my hands shake slightly as I adjust my fresh cravat, and I know with crushing certainty that our clever plan has backfired spectacularly. We sought to appear incompatible, yet instead revealed a compatibility so profound it terrifies me.

I stalk into the dining room, determined to focus on Isabel's faults. There must be some. Her stubbornness, perhaps? But no - the way her chin lifts when she's being particularly obstinate only makes me want to... No. Her sharp tongue, then. Except that every barbed comment reveals a quick wit that matches my own.

"Your soup, my lord." Winters places the bowl before me with practiced efficiency, but I catch the slight arch of his eyebrow.

I force myself to take a spoonful, though I barely taste it. What else about her? Her complete disregard for proper musical interpretation - though watching her fingers dance across the keys with such passion makes my breath catch. Her complete inability to maintain decorum in public - but Lord help me, the fire in her eyes when she argues...

"Is everything to your satisfaction, my lord?" Mrs. Hornesbury, my housekeeper, hovers nearby with unusual attentiveness.

"Quite." I snap the word more sharply than intended.

That kiss. Sweet heaven, that kiss. The way she melted against me, her lips soft yet demanding. The small whimper she made when my fingers tangled in her hair. The taste of her...

I nearly knock over my wine glass, earning another pointed look from Winters.

This is utter madness. I am Lord William Brampton. I do not moon about like some green boy experiencing his first infatuation. I manage estates. I make rational decisions. I do not sit at my own dining table imagining the curve of a woman's neck or the way her eyes flash when she's...

The door opens with a bang, and my father strides in. Thank God. Business. Duty. Something to anchor my scattered thoughts.

CHAPTER SEVEN

"William." He takes his seat, watching me with shrewd eyes. "I trust the garden party proved entertaining?"

"It was…" I search for a neutral word. "Educational."

"Indeed." He signals for his own soup. "I heard quite an educational tale about you and Lady Isabel among Lady Worthington's roses."

My spoon clatters against the bowl. "Father—"

"What game are you playing, William?" His voice carries that steel edge I remember from childhood. "The gossip is spreading through London like wildfire. Lady Isabel storming away in tears? You, following her with cutting remarks about her character?"

"Tears? It's not—"

"This match is too important to be sabotaged by whatever foolish notion has taken hold of you." He leans forward. "The joining of our estates—"

"Perhaps I don't wish to marry for estates." The words escape before I can stop them.

"Then what do you wish to marry for?" His eyes narrow. "Some romantic notion of love? I thought I raised you better than that."

The fire burning inside me flares higher. *Love?* Is that what this maddening attraction is? This consuming need to be near her, to challenge her, to make her eyes spark with that particular blend of fury and passion that sets my blood alight?

"The arguments with Lady Isabel will cease." My father's tone brooks no opposition. "You will court her properly, and you will do so immediately."

I stare at my soup, no longer seeing it. Court her properly? When every proper interaction only feeds this wild hunger for more? When simply remembering the press of her body against mine in that carriage makes my cravat feel too tight?

"Do you understand me, William?"

I look up at my father, seeing the immovable resolve in his expression. He wants me to stop fighting this match, to embrace my duty. But how can I explain that duty is no longer my greatest battle?

"Yes, Father." The words taste like ash. "I understand perfectly."

But I don't. I understand nothing. Not the way my heart races at the mere thought of her, nor how I can simultaneously dread and crave our next meeting. And I certainly don't understand how I'm supposed to stop this fire when every attempt to douse it only makes it burn hotter.

My father's voice drones on, but one phrase cuts through my distraction like a blade. "Miss Fairfax has expressed particular interest in forming an alliance with our family."

The soup turns to lead in my stomach. "Miss Fairfax?"

"Indeed." He dabs his mouth with his napkin, every movement precise and calculated. "Her father approached me at White's just this morning. Should your... difficulties with Lady Isabel persist, I have assured him we would be amenable to discussing terms."

"You cannot be serious."

"I assure you, I am entirely serious." His gray eyes fix on mine. "You will marry, William. Either Lady Isabel, with all the advantages that match brings to both our families, or Miss Fairfax, whose dowry would certainly ease our immediate financial concerns."

I push my bowl away, my appetite completely gone. *Miss Fairfax.* I've danced with her at countless balls, made the expected polite conversation. She is, without question, one of the greatest beauties of the season. Golden hair, perfect features, a figure that has half the ton's eligible men falling over themselves to gain her attention.

And yet...

I remember our last conversation at Lady Jersey's ball. She spoke at length about the weather, her new bonnet, and the latest on-dit about Lady So-and-So's scandalous choice of evening gloves. Not a single original thought passed her perfectly formed lips.

"Miss Fairfax is considered quite the catch," my father continues, watching me carefully. "Many would consider her the superior choice."

Superior? I think of Isabel's eyes flashing as she challenges my opinions on Shakespeare. The way her fingers dance across piano keys, creating music that makes my soul ache. How her quick wit matches mine step for step, turning every conversation into an intricate dance of minds.

Miss Fairfax has never read Shakespeare. She considers music a necessary accomplishment, nothing more. And wit? The closest she comes is repeating whatever clever remarks she's overheard at Almack's.

"I will not marry Miss Fairfax." The words emerge with more force than intended.

CHAPTER SEVEN

"Then you will cease this ridiculous behavior with Lady Isabel." My father's tone hardens. "No more public arguments. No more cutting remarks. No more sending her running from garden parties in tears."

"She wasn't crying," I mutter, though the thought that she might have been makes my chest tighten uncomfortably.

"You have until the end of the month to demonstrate marked improvement in your relationship with Lady Isabel. If you cannot…" He lets the threat hang in the air.

I sit back in my chair, mind racing. The thought of Isabel in another man's arms makes my blood boil. The idea of Miss Fairfax in mine leaves me cold. When did this happen? When did Isabel become so essential to my happiness?

"Do we understand each other?"

I think of Isabel's passion, her fire, the way she makes every room brighter simply by entering it. The softness of her lips against mine in that carriage, the way she challenges me to be better, to think deeper, to feel more.

"Yes, Father." I meet his gaze steadily. "We understand each other perfectly."

He nods once, satisfied, and returns to his meal. But I barely notice as the courses come and go. My mind is filled with copper-kissed hair and warm brown eyes that see straight through my carefully constructed facades. With clever remarks that make me laugh despite myself. With the way she makes my heart race and my mind spark and my very soul feel more alive.

I don't want to marry Miss Fairfax. I want Isabel. Not because of our families' expectations or the joining of our estates. But because somehow, in the midst of our elaborate charade, she has become as essential to me as breathing.

I push away from the dining table, no longer able to maintain the pretense of an appetite. My father's words about Miss Fairfax echo in my mind, but they only serve to crystallize what I've known since that moment in the carriage - Isabel was first. She claimed something in me before I even realized there was anything to claim.

"If you'll excuse me, Father." I don't wait for his response before striding from the room.

My feet carry me to the music room where Mrs. Hornesbury often plays in the evenings. The pianoforte sits silent now, but I can almost hear Isabel's music - that passionate piece she performed at the Huntington's ball.

CHAPTER SEVEN

Even then, when I'd planned to critique her playing, I couldn't deny how her fingers drew emotion from those keys that stirred something profound within me.

"She is mine." The words escape in a whisper, and their truth strikes me with physical force. Not because of our families' arrangements or society's expectations, but because no other woman has ever challenged me as she does. No other woman has matched me step for step, wit for wit, passion for passion.

I move to the window, staring out at the rain-soaked gardens. The roses where we staged our latest "argument" droop under the weight of water droplets. I remember how she looked there, sunlight catching those copper highlights in her hair, her cheeks flushed with feigned indignation. But was it entirely feigned? That flash in her eyes when she spoke of Miss Worthington...

My hands clench at my sides. The thought of Isabel believing I could be interested in another woman is unexpectedly painful. Does she not see? Can she not understand that every other woman pales in comparison to her fire, her intelligence, her sheer force of being?

"She is mine," I repeat more firmly. Not as a possession to be claimed, but as my equal - the only woman who has ever made me feel truly seen. Who strips away my carefully constructed facades with a single raised eyebrow. Who makes me want to be better, stronger, more worthy of the passion I glimpse beneath her own protective walls.

The door opens behind me, and Mrs. Hornesbury enters with her usual quiet efficiency. "My lord? Shall I play this evening?"

"No." I turn from the window. "But tell me, Mrs. Hornesbury, you were present at the Huntington's ball. What did you think of Lady Isabel's performance?"

A knowing smile touches her lips. "Her technical skill is impressive, of course, but it was her interpretation that moved me. Such passion, such understanding of the composer's intent. Almost as if she were creating the music anew with each note."

"Yes." The word comes out rougher than intended. "Exactly so."

"Though I believe someone criticized her rather harshly for that very quality." Her tone carries gentle reproach.

"A foolish man indeed." I pace the length of the room. "One who was so focused on maintaining appearances that he nearly missed the truth before him."

"And has this foolish man seen reason?"

I stop before the pianoforte, running my fingers along its polished surface. "He has realized that some things are worth more than appearances. That some connections are too precious to sacrifice for the sake of pride or schemes."

"She plays from her heart," Mrs. Hornesbury observes quietly. "Just as you manage your estates with yours, though you try to hide it behind logic and ledgers."

The truth of her words strikes deep. Isabel was first to see past my carefully maintained facade of cold efficiency. First to challenge me to show the passion I keep locked away. First to make me want more than duty and responsibility.

"She was first," I murmur, more to myself than Mrs. Hornesbury. "The first to make me feel... everything."

"Then perhaps it's time to stop pretending otherwise?"

I turn to face her, this woman who has been more mother to me than my own. "The game we've been playing... it's become real. Too real. Every barbed comment masks a compliment I long to voice. Every orchestrated argument ends with me wanting to pull her close instead of pushing her away."

"Love has a way of turning our clever plans against us."

Mrs. Hornesbury's eyes twinkle. "Especially when we try to deny it."

"Love?" The word catches in my throat. But yes, that's exactly what this is, isn't it? This fierce possessiveness, this bone-deep certainty that Isabel belongs with me, belongs to me, just as I belong to her.

"She is mine," I say for the third time, and now I understand the full weight of those words. The realization hits me with the force of a physical blow. I, Lord William Brampton, who has spent years carefully avoiding any hint of romantic entanglement, am completely, utterly, and irrevocably in love with Lady Isabel Ainsworth.

CHAPTER EIGHT
rain on my window
LADY ISABEL AINSWORTH

I stumble into my bedchamber, dripping rainwater across the Turkish carpet. My hair hangs in wet tendrils around my face, and my pale blue muslin dress clings indecently to my form. Margaret rushes forward, her eyes wide with concern.

"My lady! You're soaked through!" She hurries to help me out of my sodden garments. My fingers tremble as I try to assist her, but I can barely focus on the task. My mind keeps drifting back to the carriage, to William's arms around me, to his lips...

"What happened?" Margaret's deft hands make quick work of my stays. "Was Lord Brampton truly awful again?"

I cannot find the words to answer. How do I explain that our carefully orchestrated plan has crumbled like a house of cards? That instead of trading barbs, we traded... My cheeks flush hot at the memory.

"You're flushed, my lady. I pray you haven't caught a chill." Margaret helps me into my night rail, the soft cotton a stark contrast to my heated skin.

"No, I'm quite warm actually." *Too warm.* Every inch of my skin feels alive, tingling with awareness. Even now, I can feel the phantom press of William's fingers against my waist, the way his hand cradled my head as he kissed me.

Margaret gathers my wet things and retreats to the dressing room, leaving me alone with my tumultuous thoughts. I pace the length of my chamber, my bare feet silent on the carpet. My lips still burn from his kiss. I press my fingers to them, remembering the way he tasted of brandy and rain. The way his tongue...

I sink onto my bed, my heart racing. This was never part of the plan. We were supposed to appear incompatible, not discover that we fit together like perfectly matched puzzle pieces. The memory of his body pressed against mine makes my breath catch. The way he growled my name against my throat, his hands spanning my waist...

CHAPTER EIGHT

Rolling onto my side, I clutch my pillow to my chest. I can still feel every point where he touched me. The firm pressure of his thigh against mine as the carriage swayed. The brush of his fingers along my jaw as he tilted my face up to his. The heat of his palm through my wet dress as he pulled me closer.

I bury my face in the pillow, but it does nothing to cool my burning cheeks. I have been kissed before - chaste pecks stolen in darkened corridors during my first Season. But nothing like this. Nothing that made my whole body feel like it was aflame. Nothing that made me want to throw propriety to the wind and beg for more.

My skin prickles with awareness, remembering the way his breath felt against my neck. The low sound he made when I threaded my fingers through his hair. I squeeze my eyes shut, but that only makes the memories more vivid. The way his muscles tensed under my hands. The barely restrained power in his frame as he held me.

Rising from the bed, I move to the window. The rain still falls heavily, drumming against the glass. Lightning flashes, illuminating the grounds, and I press my forehead to the cool pane. But even the chill of the glass cannot calm the riot in my blood. Every flash of lightning reminds me of that moment when thunder crashed and I jumped into his arms. The way his eyes darkened as he looked down at me. The slight tremor in his hands as he cupped my face.

I wrap my arms around myself, trying to hold onto some semblance of control. But control seems a distant memory now. All I can think about is the way his mouth moved against mine, gentle at first, then demanding. The way my body responded without my permission, melting into his embrace. The soft moan that escaped me when his tongue traced my lower lip.

My nightrail suddenly feels too confining, too warm. I fan myself with one hand, but it does little to cool the heat burning through my veins. Every time I close my eyes, I see his face - the way he looked at me after that first kiss, shock and desire warring in his expression. The way his chest heaved as he tried to catch his breath. The slight tremor in his voice when he whispered my name.

I burrow deeper under my covers, my mind still reeling from the carriage incident. "Margaret?" I call out softly, knowing she's likely tidying my dressing room. "Would you come sit with me?"

My dear friend appears in the doorway, concern etched across her features. She settles at the foot of my bed, smoothing her apron. "What troubles you, my lady?"

CHAPTER EIGHT

"Oh Margaret, the most extraordinary thing happened today." I sit up, hugging my knees to my chest. "Lord Brampton… William… he kissed me."

Margaret's eyes widen. "He what?"

"In the carriage, during the storm. One moment we were arguing, and the next…" I touch my fingers to my lips, still feeling the ghost of his kiss. "I've never felt anything like it."

"Was it… pleasant?" Margaret leans forward, clearly intrigued.

"It was… overwhelming. Like being caught in a storm, but not wanting to seek shelter." I pause, frowning. "But then he pulled away and said he wouldn't take advantage of me. What could he have meant by that?"

Margaret tilts her head. "Perhaps he was being honorable? Ensuring he didn't compromise you?"

"But that's just it - we're already engaged! And…" I drop my voice to barely above a whisper. "I think I'm in love with him."

"But isn't that wonderful?" Margaret clasps her hands together.

"No, it's terrible! We had this ridiculous plan to appear incompatible so our fathers would break the engagement. Only now..." I flop back against my pillows. "Now I don't want it broken at all. But William clearly doesn't feel the same way. He practically fled the carriage after the kiss."

"Men can be quite dense about matters of the heart," Margaret says thoughtfully. "It reminds me of my previous position with Lady Milfred. She had the most peculiar way of handling her husband's inattention."

I prop myself up on my elbows. "What did she do?"

"She would flirt - very properly, mind you - with other gentlemen at social gatherings. Nothing scandalous, just enough to catch Lord Milford's notice. He'd become terribly jealous and suddenly couldn't lavish enough attention on her."

"And it worked?"

"Like a charm. Every time." Margaret's eyes sparkle with mischief. "Perhaps Lord Brampton needs a gentle reminder of what he stands to lose?"

I chew my lower lip, considering. "But wouldn't that be terribly manipulative?"

CHAPTER EIGHT

"More manipulative than pretending to hate each other?" Margaret raises an eyebrow. "At least this way, you're being honest about your feelings, even if he needs a little push to recognize his own."

"I suppose you have a point." I trace patterns on my counterpane. "And there is that handsome Mr. Crawford who's always so attentive at assemblies…"

"Just remember to be subtle. You want to inspire jealousy, not scandal."

"Margaret, you're brilliant." I reach out and squeeze her hand. "Though I must admit, I'm terrified. What if it doesn't work? What if he truly doesn't care for me at all?"

"My lady, I saw how he looked at you at Lady Worthington's garden party. No man looks at a woman that way if he feels nothing."

"You noticed that too?" Heat rises to my cheeks. "I thought I might have imagined it."

"Trust me, you didn't imagine anything. And the way he practically carried you to the carriage? That was not the action of a man who's indifferent."

After Margaret bids me goodnight, I nestle deeper into my bed, drawing the covers up to my chin. The steady patter of rain against my window creates a soothing rhythm that helps calm my racing thoughts. Each drop seems to echo the beating of my heart, gradually slowing it to a more manageable pace.

The storm has settled into a gentle shower now, nothing like the tempest that trapped William and me in that carriage. I close my eyes, letting the sound wash over me, trying to clear my mind of the memory of his kiss. But like water finding its way through the smallest crack, thoughts of him keep seeping back in.

No. I must focus on the task at hand. Mr. Crawford - yes, he will do nicely. He's been hovering at the edges of society gatherings, watching me with those striking blue eyes of his. The ton whispers about his reputation, but that only makes him more suitable for my purposes. William's carefully controlled facade might crack at the sight of me conversing with a known rake.

I roll onto my side, watching raindrops race down the windowpane. Mrs. Huffington's two-day dinner party presents the perfect opportunity. She always seats her guests according to their rank and connections, which means I'll likely be placed near Mr. Crawford - he may be in trade, but his wealth has earned him a place at better dinner tables. William, as the heir to an earldom, will probably be seated across from me, forced to watch every interaction.

CHAPTER EIGHT

The corners of my mouth curl up as I imagine how to play this delicate game. I'll need to be subtle - a lingering glance here, a soft laugh there. Perhaps I'll ask Mr. Crawford about his recent travels to the Continent. He's known for telling the most entertaining stories, and I can lean in just so, appearing utterly captivated by his tales.

I reach for my pillow, hugging it close as I refine my strategy. My new green silk dinner dress will be perfect - the one with the slightly daring neckline that had Father frowning in disapproval. The color brings out the copper highlights in my hair, and the cut emphasizes my figure without being scandalous.

But how to ensure Mr. Crawford takes the bait? I tap my fingers against the pillow, thinking. He's always been interested in music. Perhaps I could mention the new Italian opera scores I recently acquired. He's traveled extensively in Italy - it would be natural to seek his opinion on their authenticity.

The rain continues its gentle symphony as I map out each detail. I'll need to time everything perfectly. Too obvious, and William might see through the ruse. Too subtle, and he might not notice at all. But if I play it just right...

I sit up suddenly, struck by inspiration. The Huffington's have that magnificent new pianoforte in their music room. After dinner, when the party breaks into smaller groups, I could ask Mr. Crawford to turn pages while I play one of those Italian pieces. William won't be able to help but notice us together, heads bent over the music, sharing what appears to be an intimate moment.

Settling back against my pillows, I feel more confident in my plan. The rain has slowed to a gentle drizzle now, matching my calmer state of mind. I've always excelled at strategy games - this is just another sort of chess match, with people instead of pieces. And if my heart flutters a bit when I imagine William's reaction, well, that's merely anticipation of a plan well crafted.

I pull my blankets higher, finally feeling sleep start to creep in. As I drift off, I can almost see it playing out - William's jaw clenching as he watches Mr. Crawford lean close to whisper something in my ear, his knuckles whitening around his wine glass as I favor Crawford with a brilliant smile. *Will he remember our kiss then? Will he feel that same fire that consumed us both in the carriage?*

The last thing I hear before sleep claims me is the soft patter of rain, like nature's own applause for my carefully constructed scheme.

CHAPTER NINE
a quiet dinner party
LORD WILLIAM BRAMPTON

The chandeliers in Mrs. Huffington's dining room cast a warm glow across the polished mahogany table, highlighting the gleaming silver and crystal place settings. Fresh flower arrangements perfume the air with the scent of hothouse blooms, their delicate petals artfully arranged in towering silver epergnes. The walls, covered in rich crimson silk, reflect the candlelight and create an intimate atmosphere that makes my collar feel uncomfortably tight.

My head snaps up at the sound of laughter, clear and musical even across the crowded dining room. The Earl of Ainsworth stands at the entrance, and beside him... dear God.

Isabel glides into the room wearing an emerald silk gown that makes her copper hair glow like flames in the candlelight. The cut of her dress follows every curve with maddening precision, and the deep green brings out golden flecks in her brown eyes I'd never noticed before. My fingers tighten around my glass of claret.

"Lady Isabel, how delightful!" Mrs. Huffington rushes forward to greet them. "And looking particularly lovely this evening."

I straighten my shoulders, preparing for Isabel to acknowledge me as propriety demands. After all, our engagement may be a sham, but appearances must be maintained. Yet she sweeps past without so much as a glance in my direction, accepting compliments from the assembled guests with graceful nods.

The devil take her. I'd planned to ignore her myself tonight, but being beaten to the slight stings more than it should. I force my attention back to Lord Pembroke's discourse on crop rotation, though my eyes keep tracking her movement through the room.

She circles the gathering like a shark in silk, always managing to remain just within my peripheral vision without ever directly approaching. The candlelight catches on the

CHAPTER NINE

emerald drops at her ears when she tilts her head to laugh at someone's jest. My jaw clenches. The sound pierces straight through me, and I have to resist the urge to stride across the room and pull her into my arms, propriety be damned.

"I say, Brampton, you seem rather distracted this evening." Lord Rutherford's voice breaks through my increasingly improper thoughts. Thank God for the interruption.

"Not at all," I lie smoothly, turning to give him my full attention. "You were saying something about your new breeding program for hunters?"

But even as Rutherford launches into his favorite topic, I remain acutely aware of Isabel's presence. The rustle of her skirts as she passes behind me. The subtle scent of lavender water that lingers in her wake. The musical cadence of her voice drifting over from where she now stands with a cluster of young ladies, deliberately angled to show me her profile.

The minx knows exactly what she's doing. And blast it all, but it's working. Every fiber of my being strains toward her while I maintain my pose of polite attention to Rutherford's discourse. My fingers itch to trace the elegant line of her neck, to tangle in those copper curls that have escaped their pins to brush tantalizingly against her bare shoulders.

"Fascinating breeding lines," I manage to interject at what seems an appropriate moment, though I haven't heard a word Rutherford said. Isabel's laugh rings out again, and I nearly crush the delicate crystal stem of my wine glass.

The room has grown insufferably warm. I tug at my cravat, trying to ease the constriction around my throat. Rutherford drones on about bloodlines and confirmation, but all I can focus on is the way Isabel's gown clings to her waist as she turns, the flash of a trim ankle beneath her hem as she steps forward, the curve of her throat as she tips her head back.

"Capital idea about the Arabian cross," I say automatically when Rutherford pauses for breath. In truth, I have no idea what breeding scheme he's proposing. All my faculties are occupied with not staring at Isabel like some green boy at his first Assembly. She knows precisely what effect she's having - I can see it in the slight quirk of her lips when she glances past me, pretending not to notice my presence while ensuring I notice hers.

I maintain my position near Lord Rutherford, discussing the latest developments in steam-powered farming

CHAPTER NINE

equipment, but my attention keeps drifting to Isabel across the room. She stands near the fireplace, her green silk gown catching the firelight in a way that makes her appear to glow. But it's not her beauty that draws my eye now—it's the man beside her.

John Crawford leans close to whisper something in her ear, and Isabel's responding laugh sends an unexpected surge of heat through my chest. The rake's reputation precedes him, yet Isabel appears utterly charmed by whatever scandalous nonsense he's sharing.

"Don't you agree, Lord Brampton?" Lord Rutherford's question pulls me back to our conversation.

"Indeed," I respond smoothly, though I haven't heard a word he's said. My fingers tighten around my glass as Crawford's hand brushes Isabel's arm in a gesture far too familiar for proper society.

When Mrs. Huffington announces dinner, I escort Lady Pembroke to the dining room, carefully avoiding looking in Isabel's direction. But once seated, I find myself directly across from her, with Crawford to her left. The first course arrives—some sort of cold soup—but I barely taste it.

"Mr. Crawford," Isabel's voice carries clearly across the table, "you must tell everyone about your adventures in

Greece. The story about the fishing boat was particularly thrilling."

Crawford preens under her attention. "My dear Lady Isabel, I wouldn't wish to bore the company—"

"Oh, but you must! Your storytelling is absolutely captivating."

My soup spoon clinks against the bowl with more force than necessary. The vapid conversation continues, punctuated by Isabel's musical laughter and Crawford's increasingly bold compliments. Other guests begin exchanging knowing looks—even Mrs. Huffington appears concerned by the display.

"William." My father's voice, low and stern, draws my attention. "Miss Fairfax has been asking after you. Perhaps you should call on her tomorrow."

I meet his steel-blue gaze, identical to my own, and notice the warning there. He's observed Isabel's behavior as well, and his meaning is clear: if one marriage prospect proves unsuitable, another can be arranged.

The fish course arrives, but the perfectly cooked sole might as well be sawdust in my mouth. Isabel leans closer to Crawford, her eyes sparkling as she hangs on his every word. My hand clenches around my wine glass, and I force myself to relax my grip before I shatter the crystal.

"The Mediterranean sunshine is incomparable," Crawford declares, clearly warming to his audience. "Though I dare say it pales in comparison to Lady Isabel's radiant presence."

Several guests titter at his boldness. Isabel's cheeks flush becomingly, and she drops her gaze to her plate in a show of modesty that I know is entirely false. I've seen her true nature—the sharp wit, the fierce intelligence she tries to hide. This coy creature before me is as much an act as our previous sparring matches, but for whose benefit?

The answer hits me with the force of a physical blow. She's deliberately drawing Crawford's attention, encouraging his infamous reputation for dalliance. But why? To make me jealous? To force our fathers to break the engagement? Or perhaps...she genuinely enjoys his attention?

The thought sits like lead in my stomach as the dinner continues. I maintain my composure, responding appropriately to Lady Pembroke's attempts at conversation, but my awareness never strays from the pair across the table. Every laugh, every shared glance, every "accidental" touch of hands feels like a personal affront.

"I hear you're quite the horsewoman, Lady Isabel," Crawford says, his voice carrying that particular tone that makes everything sound like an innuendo. "Perhaps you'd allow me to accompany you on a ride through the park tomorrow morning?"

Before Isabel can respond, my father clears his throat meaningfully. "I believe Lady Isabel already has commitments tomorrow morning. Isn't that right, Ainsworth?"

Lord Ainsworth startles slightly, clearly caught off guard. "Oh! Yes, quite right. Family obligations, you understand."

I take a sip of wine to hide my satisfaction at Crawford's thwarted attempt, but the feeling is short-lived as Isabel gives him a look of such apparent disappointment that my teeth clench of their own accord.

After the interminable dinner, Mrs. Huffington herds us into the music room like prized sheep. The space, though generous, feels stifling with the press of bodies and the heat of too many candles. Isabel deliberately positions herself across the room, settling onto a silk-covered settee beside Crawford. His arm drapes across the back, not quite touching her shoulders but suggesting an intimacy that makes my blood boil.

The Italian soprano Mrs. Huffington has engaged launches into an aria from Mozart's "Le Nozze di Figaro." Under normal circumstances, I might appreciate the technical precision of her performance, but tonight every note grates against my nerves. Especially when Crawford leans close to whisper something in Isabel's ear during a particularly moving passage, earning him a swift elbow from his other seatmate, the ever-proper Lady Rutherford.

A commotion at the door draws attention from the performance. The Fairfaxs sweep in, fashionably late from Lady Jersey's rout. Miss Fairfax's blonde curls bounce as she offers profuse apologies for the interruption. Providence has provided me with the perfect opportunity for retaliation.

I rise smoothly from my seat and bow. "Miss Fairfax, allow me to secure you a better view." I guide her to an empty chair near the front, positioned where Isabel cannot help but notice us.

"How fortunate we are to catch such exquisite entertainment," I murmur, pitching my voice to carry just far enough. "Though I confess, your presence enhances the evening considerably."

Miss Fairfax preens under the attention, her fan fluttering rapidly. "Lord Brampton, you flatter me shamelessly."

"Merely speaking truth, I assure you." I lean closer, noting with satisfaction how Isabel shifts restlessly in her seat. "That shade of blue suits you admirably. It brings out the celestial quality of your eyes."

The soprano reaches a particularly impressive high note, but I keep my focus on Miss Fairfaix's simpering response. From the corner of my eye, I see Isabel's fingers clench in her skirts. Crawford attempts to recapture her attention, but she appears distracted, her gaze repeatedly darting in our direction.

"I understand you're quite accomplished at the pianoforte," I continue, though I have no such knowledge. "Perhaps you might favor us with a performance after Madame concludes?"

"Oh! I couldn't possibly..." Miss Fairfax demurs, though her expression suggests she's already selecting a piece to play.

"I insist." I capture her hand and press it warmly. "Your modesty does you credit, but surely you won't deny us such a pleasure?"

CHAPTER NINE

A sharp movement draws my attention. Isabel stands abruptly, causing Lady Rutherford to start in surprise. She murmurs something to her father and sweeps from the room, her spine rigid with what I hope is jealousy. Crawford half-rises to follow, but Lord Ainsworth's quelling look keeps him in his seat.

"I fear Lady Isabel is unwell," Miss Fairfax observes with false concern. "Perhaps the evening's excitement has overcome her?"

"Indeed." I maintain my expression of polite interest, though satisfaction courses through me. "Now, about that performance..."

The soprano concludes her aria to enthusiastic applause. As Miss Fairfax makes her way to the pianoforte, I catch my father's approving nod. He clearly believes I've taken his hint about pursuing alternative marriage prospects. Let him think so—it serves my purpose for now.

But my thoughts remain with Isabel, imagining her face as she fled the room. The flash of hurt in those expressive brown eyes. The tight press of her lips. The way her hands trembled slightly as she gathered her skirts.

Miss Fairfax begins a popular ballad, her technique competent but uninspired. Nothing like the passion

Isabel brings to her playing, the way her entire being seems to flow into the music. I shake off the comparison. Tonight has proved that our little scheme has become far more complicated than either of us anticipated.

CHAPTER TEN
the pianoforte
LADY ISABEL AINSWORTH

I slip into Mrs. Huffington's morning room, my hands trembling as I shut the heavy oak door behind me. The silk of my gown rustles as I sink onto a delicate settee, pressing my palms against my burning cheeks. Curse William Brampton and his insufferable composure. Not once - not a single time during dinner - did he even glance in my direction when I spoke with Mr. Crawford. Instead, he seemed entirely captivated by Miss Fairfax's vapid observations about the weather.

I pace the morning room, my fingers twisting the delicate lace of my handkerchief. The evening had been an unmitigated disaster. My brilliant scheme to provoke William's jealousy by entertaining Mr. Crawford's attentions has failed spectacularly. Instead of the burning glares I'd anticipated, William maintained that insufferable mask of aristocratic indifference throughout dinner.

"Absolutely fascinating, Mr. Crawford," I'd simpered, forcing a laugh at yet another of his questionable jests. The sound had rung hollow in my own ears, and I'd caught Mrs. Huffington's raised eyebrow from across the table. But William? He'd merely lifted his wine glass, his attention fixed on Miss Rutherford's endless prattling about her new bonnet.

My stomach churns at the memory of his slight smile as he leaned closer to hear her whispered commentary. What could she possibly have said to merit such interest? The woman can hardly string two thoughts together without pausing to adjust her perfectly arranged curls.

I stop before the gilt-framed mirror, studying my reflection. My cheeks are flushed with frustration, and a rebellious curl has escaped its pins. "Perhaps I'm going about this all wrong," I murmur to my reflection.

Mr. Crawford's increasingly bold behavior is becoming problematic. His hand had "accidentally" brushed mine three times during dinner, and his gaze had lingered far too long on the neckline of my gown. The thought of encouraging his advances any further makes my skin crawl. But what choice do I have? William seems determined to ignore my existence entirely.

"Lady Isabel?" Mr. Crawford's voice carries through the door, and I stiffen. "Are you quite well? You left the drawing room rather abruptly."

I press my lips together, fighting the urge to tell him precisely where he can direct his concern. Instead, I smooth my skirts and adopt what I hope is a convincing tone of distress. "Just a momentary spell, Mr. Crawford. I shall rejoin the party shortly."

"Perhaps I might offer you some assistance?" The door handle rattles, and I dart forward to ensure the latch is secure.

"That won't be necessary!" My voice rises sharply, and I wince at the breach in decorum. "I mean to say, I simply require a moment of solitude."

Through the door, I hear William's deep voice, and my heart leaps traitorously in my chest. But he's speaking to Miss Fairfax again, their conversation a muted murmur in the hallway. The sound of their shared laughter feels like a physical blow.

I sink onto a nearby chair, pressing my fingers to my temples. *What does he see in her?* Yes, she's pretty enough in that insipid, conventional way the ton seems to favor. But surely William, with his razor-sharp wit and scholarly interests, must be bored senseless by her endless chatter about ribbons and the latest on-dits?

Unless... unless he truly means to cry off our engagement? The thought sends an unexpected shaft of pain through my chest. Was our kiss in the carriage so meaningless to him? I'd felt the tremor in his hands, the racing of his heart beneath my palms. Surely that wasn't merely skilled acting?

"This is intolerable," I whisper to the empty room. My original plan to appear unsuitable seems laughably naive now. Instead of driving William away, I find myself desperate for even a moment of his attention. When did everything become so complicated?

The sound of Miss Fairfax's tittering laugh drifts through the door again, and I clench my hands in my lap. William's answering chuckle makes my blood boil. He hasn't spoken a single word to me all evening - not even the cutting remarks we'd previously exchanged with such relish. His complete indifference is far worse than any calculated insult.

I stand abruptly, smoothing my skirts with trembling hands. This cannot continue. Either William is truly

CHAPTER TEN

indifferent to me - in which case I must steel my heart against this inconvenient attraction - or he is playing some game of his own. Either way, I cannot spend another moment hiding in this room while he flirts with that simpering miss.

A tear escapes despite my best efforts to maintain composure. I dash it away with angry fingers, smudging what remains of my carefully applied rouge.

The door opens with a soft click, and I straighten immediately, preparing an excuse for my absence. But it's Mrs. Huffington herself who enters, her kind face creased with concern.

"My dear girl," she says, producing a delicate handkerchief from her sleeve. "Here now, dry those lovely eyes."

"I apologize for hiding away in your morning room," I manage, accepting the offered cloth. "I needed a moment to... collect myself."

Mrs. Huffington settles beside me, her silk skirts whispering against mine. "There's no need for apologies. Though I must say, your attempts to draw Lord Brampton's attention through Mr. Crawford might have been more effective if Miss Fairfax weren't in attendance."

I feel my cheeks flame anew. "Was I so transparent?"

"Only to those who know what to look for." She pats my hand. "But I'm afraid I must tell you something that's been making its way through London's drawing rooms."

My stomach tightens. "Please, do not spare my feelings."

"The Earl of Brampton - William's father - has already begun negotiations with Fairfax. Should your engagement fail..." She trails off, but the meaning is clear.

The room spins slightly, and I grip the edge of the settee. "He means to marry William to Miss Fairfax?"

"The contracts are apparently drawn up, merely awaiting signatures."

My heart feels as though it's being crushed in a vice. "What am I to do? I cannot bear to watch him with her, knowing..."

Mrs. Huffington's eyes spark with sudden inspiration. "My dear, I have endured Miss Fairfax's massacre of Mozart for the past quarter hour. Why don't you show Lord Brampton exactly what he would be giving up?"

"Through music?" I whisper.

"Through everything. Your talent, your grace, your passion. I've heard you play at Almack's - you have a gift

CHAPTER TEN

that goes beyond mere technical skill." She stands, extending her hand to help me rise. "Come. Dry your eyes, fix your powder, and remind that young man what real music sounds like. And perhaps..." She smiles conspiratorially. "Perhaps remind him what real feeling looks like as well."

I allow her to help me to my feet, smoothing my skirts with trembling hands. "But what if—"

"No 'what ifs,' my dear. I saw how he watched you during dinner, when he thought no one was looking. That was not the gaze of a man indifferent to his dinner companion's flirtations." She produces a small powder compact from her reticule. "Now, let me help you repair these tears, and then we shall return to the drawing room. I believe Beethoven's Moonlight Sonata would be particularly appropriate, don't you think?"

I glide back into the drawing room, my spine straight as a sword blade despite the trembling in my hands. The remnants of my tears have been carefully powdered away, though my heart still thunders against my ribs. Miss Fairfax's tepid performance has mercifully concluded, leaving the pianoforte blessedly empty.

Several guests linger near the refreshment table, their quiet conversations punctuated by the gentle clink of crystal. Mr. Crawford starts to rise from his seat, no doubt intending to intercept my path, but I sweep past him without acknowledgment. The polished wood of the piano bench is cool beneath my skirts as I settle myself, adjusting my posture with practiced grace.

My fingers hover over the keys for a heartbeat or two. Then I begin, letting the first notes of Beethoven's Moonlight Sonata drift into the air like midnight mist. The opening measures flow soft and dream-like, with each note perfectly weighted. This is no mere performance piece to showcase technical skill—it is my soul laid bare through music.

As the melody builds, weaving its spell through the room, I hear the rustle of silk and wool as guests begin to return. Their footsteps pause, then settle into the available chairs. I keep my focus on the keys, letting the music speak what my lips cannot.

The piece grows in intensity, my fingers drawing forth waves of sound that crash and recede like an ocean tide. This is how it feels to love him—this terrible, wonderful ache that threatens to consume me whole. Each phrase carries the weight of unspoken words, stolen glances, and forbidden touches.

CHAPTER TEN

As the room fills, more chairs scrape quietly against the floor. I pour everything into the music—my frustration, my longing, my fear of losing him to another. The melody soars and plunges, and I with it, until there is nothing else in the world but these notes and the story they tell.

A subtle shift in the air tells me the moment William enters. I don't need to look up to know he's there, watching from the back of the room. My fingers never falter as they dance across the keys, though my pulse quickens traitorously. Let him watch. Let him see what passion truly looks like, not the pale imitation Miss Fairfax offers.

The final movement flows from my hands like liquid moonlight. I think of our kiss in the carriage, of thunder and rain and the taste of his lips. The music swells with remembered desire, then gentles into something achingly tender. This is what we could be, William, if you would only see it.

As the last notes fade into silence, I remain still, hands resting lightly on the keys. The room stays hushed for several heartbeats before erupting into enthusiastic applause. I rise and curtsey, accepting their praise with a small smile that doesn't quite reach my eyes.

Only then do I allow myself to look toward the back of the room. William stands apart from the others, his face half in shadow. But I catch the intensity of his gaze, the slight parting of his lips, the way his hands are clenched at his sides. His eyes follow Mr. Crawford's approach to the piano, and I see something dark flash across his features.

The other guests press forward with their compliments, but I barely hear them. In this moment, there is only William, and the unspoken symphony between us that threatens to drown out everything else.

Mrs. Huffington appears at my elbow, her eyes twinkling with satisfaction. "My dear, you've quite outdone yourself. I believe everyone here has been thoroughly reminded of your extraordinary talent."

I accept her praise with another curtsey, though my attention remains fixed on William's tall figure as he turns and strides from the room. His departure should feel like defeat, but somehow it doesn't. Because in that brief moment when our eyes met, I saw something that gave me hope - something that looked remarkably like surrender.

CHAPTER ELEVEN
passion erupts
LADY ISABEL AINSWORTH

The final notes of Beethoven's Moonlight Sonata fade beneath my fingers as applause erupts around me. I rise from the pianoforte, offering a modest curtsy to the gathered admirers. Their praise washes over me yet feels hollow without the one person whose opinion I truly desire.

"Exquisite, Lady Isabel," the Earl of Brampton's deep voice cuts through the chatter. "I have not heard such mastery since your mother's performances."

I force a gracious smile. "You honor me with such a comparison, my lord."

More compliments follow, but my eyes scan the room, searching for a tall figure with golden hair. Where has

William disappeared to? The crowd around me shifts and moves, but he is conspicuously absent.

Mrs. Huffington appears at my elbow, her silk skirts rustling. "You must be parched, my dear. Come, let us find you some refreshment."

She guides me through the throng to a table laden with delicate glasses of ratafia and small confections. Before I can select a drink, she squeezes my hand and melts away into the crowd, leaving me oddly bereft.

"Lady Isabel." Mr. Crawford's smooth voice startles me. He has materialized at my side, far closer than propriety dictates. "Your performance was... transcendent."

"You are too kind, sir." I accept the glass he offers, noting how his fingers brush mine in a way that cannot be accidental.

"Not at all. Such talent deserves recognition." His blue eyes hold mine with an intensity that should make me uncomfortable, yet I find myself warming to his attention. "The way your hands move across the keys... one could watch for hours."

A laugh escapes me – small and perhaps a touch brittle, but genuine nonetheless. "Surely you exaggerate, Mr. Crawford."

CHAPTER ELEVEN

"I assure you, I do not." He steps closer still, his voice dropping to an intimate murmur. "Beauty combined with such skill is... intoxicating."

The compliment soothes something raw within me, even as I know it should not. His attention is a balm to my wounded pride, and I allow myself to bask in it, if only for a moment. My smile comes easier now, though it masks the ache in my chest.

A flash of movement catches my eye, and my breath catches. Across the room, William stands with Miss Fairfax, their heads bent close in conversation. Her fan flutters coyly as she gazes up at him, and his lips curve in that half-smile I once thought reserved for me alone. They make a striking pair – her golden curls matching his own, her delicate features lifted in obvious admiration.

"Lady Isabel?" Mr. Crawford's voice draws me back. "Are you well? You've gone quite pale."

I lift my chin, determined not to let my distress show. "Perfectly well, I assure you. The room is merely warm after my exertions at the pianoforte."

"Then perhaps you would benefit from a turn about the room?" He offers his arm with a gallant flourish.

I place my hand upon his sleeve, grateful for the distraction. "Thank you, sir. That would be lovely."

As we begin our promenade, I force myself to focus on Mr. Crawford's pleasant conversation rather than the couple in the corner. His wit is sharp, his observations amusing, and if his compliments are perhaps too forward, well – who am I to judge? At least someone finds me worthy of pursuit.

"You must allow me to call upon you," he murmurs as we complete our circuit. "I should very much like to hear you play again... in a more intimate setting."

The impropriety of his suggestion should shock me, but I find myself considering it. My eyes drift once more to William and Miss Fairfax, still deep in their private discourse. The sight of his hand touching her arm as he makes some point sends a fresh wave of pain through my chest.

"What a fascinating observation, Mr. Crawford." I tilt my head and let my laugh ring out, perhaps a touch louder than strictly necessary. My fingers trail along his sleeve as we position ourselves near the refreshment table – directly in William's line of sight.

"You flatter me, Lady Isabel." Mr. Crawford leans closer, his breath warm against my ear. "Though I speak nothing but truth when I say your beauty outshines every lady in this room."

I feel William's attention shift before I see it. The weight of his gaze burns against my skin even as I keep my focus steadfastly on Mr. Crawford's admittedly handsome face. "Such pretty words, sir. Do you practice them before a mirror?"

"Only when I know I shall be in your presence." His hand brushes mine as he takes my empty glass, replacing it with a fresh one. The touch lingers longer than proper.

From the corner of my eye, I see William's jaw tighten. Yet instead of approaching, he bends to whisper something to Miss Fairfax that makes her titter behind her fan. My stomach twists.

"Tell me more about your travels abroad, Mr. Crawford." I step marginally closer, pitching my voice to carry. "I find myself fascinated by your adventures in Venice."

"The canals pale in comparison to your eyes, my lady." His fingers ghost across my wrist, and I suppress a shiver – though not entirely from pleasure. "Though I would gladly describe every detail if it means keeping your attention."

A sharp laugh cuts through our exchange – Miss Fairfax's artificial trill. I turn just enough to see William's hand at her waist as he guides her toward the pianoforte. My teeth clench behind my smile.

"Perhaps we might find somewhere more... private to continue our discussion?" Mr. Crawford suggests, his tone heavy with implication.

Before I can respond, William's voice rings out. "Miss Fairfax has agreed to favor us with a performance."

Oh no, not again...

The first discordant notes make me wince. Her fingers stumble across the keys in a manner that would make any music master weep. Yet William stands beside her, nodding encouragingly as she massacres Mozart for a second time.

"Shall we move closer to better appreciate the... music?" Mr. Crawford's hand settles at the small of my back, guiding me forward.

I allow it, though my skin crawls at his presumption. "What a... unique interpretation," I murmur, just loud enough to carry.

William's head snaps up, his eyes meeting mine with such intensity I nearly step back. But then Miss Fairfax

CHAPTER ELEVEN

hits a particularly sour note, and he returns his attention to her, his smile never wavering.

"I much preferred your performance," Mr. Crawford whispers, his lips nearly brushing my ear. "Such passion, such... skill."

I feel rather than see William stiffen. His hands clench behind his back, though his expression remains perfectly pleasant as Miss Fairfax continues her assault on the instrument.

"You are too kind." I touch Mr. Crawford's arm, letting my fingers linger. "Though I fear I cannot take credit for natural talent."

"Nonsense." He captures my hand, his thumb stroking my palm in a wholly inappropriate manner. "Your... talents are evident in everything you do."

The music stops abruptly. William's voice cuts through the awkward silence. "Magnificent, Miss Fairfax. Your dedication to the art is... apparent."

She preens under his praise, and something snaps inside me. I turn fully toward Mr. Crawford, pitching my voice to carry. "Perhaps we might find that quieter spot you mentioned? I should love to hear more about your travels."

"Lady Isabel." William's voice cracks like a whip, though when I glance over, he's still focused on Miss Fairfax. "I believe your father was looking for you earlier."

"How fortunate then, that I am easily found." I step closer to Mr. Crawford, noting how William's shoulders tense. "Though I wouldn't want to abandon such charming company."

The room crackles with tension as William finally turns to face us fully. His eyes, normally so carefully controlled, blaze with something dangerous. Miss Fairfax touches his arm, but he shakes her off, taking a step in our direction.

My breath catches as William stalks toward me, his expression thunderous. The guests part before him like waves breaking against a cliff, and I lift my chin in defiance even as my heart pounds against my ribs.

"Lady Isabel." His voice is deceptively soft. "A word, if you please."

"I am otherwise engaged, my lord." I gesture to Mr. Crawford, who has not relinquished his hold on my hand.

William's eyes drop to our joined hands, and something dangerous flashes across his face. "I insist."

CHAPTER ELEVEN

"And I decline." The words emerge sharper than intended. "Surely Miss Fairfax's company is more agreeable?"

"Do not test me." He steps closer, close enough that I can smell the bergamot on his skin. "Not in this."

Heat rises to my cheeks. "I was unaware I required your permission to converse with guests."

"You do when the gentleman in question has designs far beyond mere conversation." His jaw clenches. "Or perhaps that was your intention?"

"How dare you!" I wrench my hand from Mr. Crawford's grasp and face William fully. "You have no right—"

"I have *every* right." The words explode from him, echoing through the suddenly silent room. "Or have you forgotten our arrangement?"

"Forgotten?" I laugh, the sound brittle. "How could I, when you remind me of my duty at every turn? Though you seem to have no trouble seeking alternative arrangements."

His eyes narrow. "What precisely are you implying?"

"Only that Miss Fairfax appears quite comfortable with your... *attention*."

The crowd around us draws back further, forming a circle of avid spectators. I spot Mrs. Huffington's concerned face among them, but I cannot stop now.

"You know nothing of my intentions toward Miss Fairfax." William's voice drops dangerously low.

"And you know nothing of mine toward Mr. Crawford." I toss my head, aware of every eye upon us. "Though perhaps you should consider his attentions a blessing. It would simplify matters for everyone, would it not?"

In two swift strides, William closes the distance between us. His hands grasp my upper arms, and suddenly I'm pressed against the solid wall of his chest. The room collectively gasps.

"Enough." His breath fans across my face, his eyes boring into mine. "This game ends *now*."

I struggle against his grip, though not truly wanting to break free. "What game? I merely follow your example—"

"Damn my example!" His fingers flex against my skin. "And damn your stubborn pride. Do you think I cannot see through this charade?"

"William!" The Earl of Brampton's voice cracks through

CHAPTER ELEVEN

the tension. "Release Lady Isabel this instant. You forget yourself, sir."

William's grip loosens, but he does not step back. If anything, he draws me closer, his eyes never leaving mine. The heat of his body seeps through my gown, making it difficult to think clearly.

"No, Father." William's voice rings out clear and strong. "For the first time, I believe I remember *exactly* who I am."

The Earl strides forward, his face dark with fury. "You will explain yourself immediately."

William finally tears his gaze from mine to face his father. "What explanation is needed? Isabel is my betrothed, and I intend to marry her."

"After this display?" The Earl's voice drips with disdain. "You have made a spectacle of yourself—of both families."

"Then let me make my intentions perfectly clear." William's arm slides around my waist, anchoring me to his side. His voice rises, addressing the entire room. "Lady Isabel Ainsworth is mine. Any gentleman harboring designs upon her person or affections would do well to remember that fact."

Mr. Crawford steps forward, his face flushed. "My lord, if you think—"

"I think, sir," William cuts him off with deadly precision, "that you were just leaving."

The tension crackles between them until Mr. Crawford finally bows stiffly and retreats. I remain frozen against William's side, my heart thundering so loudly I'm certain everyone must hear it.

"As for the rest," William continues, his grip tightening possessively, "let there be no confusion. I *will* marry Isabel, and any whispers of alternative arrangements are not only false… but unwelcome."

CHAPTER TWELVE
proclaimed intention
LORD WILLIAM BRAMPTON

I stare at the ceiling of my bedchamber, watching the morning light creep across the ornate moldings. My head pounds with the remnants of last night's brandy - far too much of it consumed after that disastrous display at the Huffington's dinner party.

What came over me? The memory of Isabel's smile directed at Crawford sends a fresh wave of anger through my chest. Her tinkling laugh, the way she leaned toward him, how her eyes sparkled with... No. I press my palms against my eyes until spots dance in the darkness.

I drag myself from bed, wincing at the brightness streaming through the windows. My valet Thompson has already laid out my morning clothes, but I wave him away when he appears to assist me. I need solitude to sort through the chaos in my mind.

Isabel's performance last night... The way her fingers danced across the keys, how her entire being seemed to merge with the music. She was transcendent, glowing with an inner light that made it impossible to look away. The piece she chose - Beethoven's Moonlight Sonata - spoke of such longing, such depth of feeling. I had to flee the room before anyone noticed how deeply it affected me.

"Coward," I mutter, yanking my cravat into place with more force than necessary. That's when Miss Fairfax appeared, chattering about her own modest musical abilities. I seized upon her presence like a drowning man clutching a rope, letting her idle conversation wash over me while my treacherous heart continued to race from Isabel's performance.

My fingers drum restlessly against the windowpane as I stare out at the morning mist shrouding the gardens. This unfamiliar ache in my chest refuses to subside. I've experienced attraction before, even infatuation, but this... *this* is different. The very thought of Isabel makes my breath catch, my skin tingle with awareness. When she smiles - truly smiles, not those polite society expressions -

dimples appear in her cheeks and her eyes sparkle with mischief.

"Stop this immediately," I command myself, pacing the length of my chamber. "You're behaving like a green boy experiencing his first crush."

But the memory of her persists - the graceful curve of her neck as she bent over the pianoforte, the way her copper-kissed curls escaped their pins during particularly passionate passages, how her chest rose and fell with quick breaths when she finished playing...

I grab my decanter of brandy, then set it down again untouched. More spirits will not solve this predicament. This foreign sensation coursing through my veins - surely it cannot be what I fear it is. Love is for poets and romance novels, not for men who bear the weight of an earldom on their shoulders.

Yet I cannot deny how my heart clenches when Crawford stands too close to her, or how my fingers itch to brush away the loose curls that frame her face. The urge to claim her, to announce to all of society that she belongs with me - it grows stronger by the day.

"She was supposed to be unsuitable," I groan, dropping into my desk chair. "This was meant to be a simple plan to avoid an unwanted marriage. When did it become so damnably complicated?"

The answer whispers through my mind: It became complicated the moment I first saw her, though I was too stubborn to admit it. The spark in her eyes when she challenges me, the quick wit that matches my own, the passion she pours into everything she does - even her attempts to appear difficult only make her more appealing.

I pull out a fresh sheet of paper, determined to list all the reasons why this attraction is foolish. My pen hovers over the blank page, but no words come. Instead, my mind fills with images of Isabel - her laugh when she thinks no one is watching, the grace of her movements, the fire in her eyes when she's angry.

"This is madness," I mutter, crumpling the paper. "Complete and utter madness."

How does one banish feelings that have taken root so deeply? The very thought of her marrying Crawford makes me want to challenge the man to a duel. The possibility of her being claimed by another... my hands clench into fists at my sides.

"Your morning tea, my lord." Peters enters with practiced silence, setting down the silver tray.

CHAPTER TWELVE

I grunt in acknowledgment but make no move to rise. The thought of facing society after my barbaric display makes my stomach turn. To grab Isabel like some untutored stable boy, to practically announce my... my what? My desire? My possession?

"The Earl requests your presence at breakfast, my lord."

Of course he does. Father witnessed the entire spectacle. The great Lord Brampton, losing all sense of propriety over a woman who clearly delights in tormenting me. I swing my legs over the side of the bed, wincing as my bare feet hit the cold floor.

"Tell him I'll be down shortly."

As Peters helps me dress, my mind keeps returning to the moment Crawford's fingers brushed Isabel's arm. The rage that flooded my veins was... unprecedented. I've never lost control like that. Not once in all my years of careful training and rigid self-discipline.

"Your cravat, my lord?" Peters holds up two options.

"The blue." I need every scrap of dignity I can muster today.

The morning paper sits unopened on my desk, and I know without looking that our scene will feature prominently in the society pages. The ton lives for such scandals. Lord Brampton, the very model of propriety, publicly claiming his unwilling bride-to-be while she openly flirts with London's most notorious rake.

I pause before my mirror, adjusting my already perfect cravat. The man staring back looks composed, controlled - everything I failed to be last night. But his eyes... there's something wild there I've never noticed before. Something that emerged the moment I saw Crawford lean close to whisper in Isabel's ear.

"Blast." I slam my palm against the wall, making Peters jump. "My apologies."

The walk to the breakfast room feels interminable. Each servant I pass seems to be hiding a knowing smile. They all witnessed my return last night, storming through the halls like some gothic hero in a penny dreadful.

What must Isabel think of me now? The thought stops me cold in the corridor. Our careful plan to appear unsuitable lies in ruins, thanks to my inexcusable behavior. Instead of demonstrating our incompatibility, I proclaimed my intention to marry her before half of London society.

And yet... the memory of her eyes when I pulled her close... There had been anger there, yes, but something

CHAPTER TWELVE

else too. Something that matched the fire burning in my own chest.

"William." Father's voice cuts through my reverie as I enter the breakfast room. "Sit."

I take my usual chair, noting the tight set of his jaw. He hasn't looked this severe since catching me climbing out my bedroom window at sixteen.

"I trust you've had time to reflect on your behavior last night?"

"Yes, sir." I reach for the coffee, desperate for something to do with my hands.

"Your display was..." He pauses, searching for words strong enough to convey his disappointment. "Unprecedented. Unseemly. Entirely beneath your station."

Each word lands like a physical blow. He's right, of course. Everything about last night was beneath me. The jealousy, the possessiveness, the public claiming of a woman who has made it abundantly clear she wants nothing to do with me.

"However." Father sets down his cup with precise movements. "It seems your outburst may have served some purpose after all."

I look up sharply.

"Crawford's interest in Isabel was becoming... problematic. Your declaration has made your position clear. No gentleman would dare pursue her now."

The satisfaction in his voice makes my skin crawl. Is that what I've done? Marked my territory like some rutting stag? The thought of Isabel's reaction to being thus claimed makes me want to crawl under the table and hide.

"The Fairfax connection is now, of course, completely impossible." Father continues as if discussing the weather. "But perhaps that's for the best. Your behavior made it quite clear where your... interests lie."

I agree wholeheartedly, wishing the night's events were nothing but a fevered dream conjured by too much brandy. The weight of what I've done - marking Isabel as mine so publicly, so crudely - sits like lead in my stomach. This was never how I intended matters to progress.

"The wedding will proceed as planned." Father's words hit me like a physical blow. "Next Friday, to be precise. The Earl of Ainsworth sent word this morning."

CHAPTER TWELVE

My coffee cup rattles against its saucer. Next Friday? So soon? I had thought we would have more time to... to what? Continue this elaborate charade that had already spectacularly backfired?

"You will, of course, cease this public sparring with Lady Isabel immediately." Father's tone brooks no argument. "We cannot afford another display like last night's performance."

"Is that all you care about?" The words burst from me before I can stop them. "Our precious family name?"

Father's face hardens, then does something unexpected – it softens. He sets down his paper and removes his reading glasses, a gesture so uncharacteristic I find myself holding my breath.

"I loved your mother," he says quietly. The admission stuns me into silence. In all my four and twenty years, I have never heard him speak of her thus. "In my own way. But she..." His voice catches. "She died before I could tell her so."

I stare at him, trying to reconcile this vulnerable man with the stern patriarch I've known all my life. "Father, I—"

"No, let me finish." He polishes his glasses with methodical precision. "I see how you look at Lady Isabel. It's the same way I looked at your mother, though I was too proud to show it. Don't make my mistake, William. Show her affection, not discord."

The irony of his advice, given our deliberate scheme to appear unsuitable, would be laughable if it weren't so painful. But perhaps he's right. After last night, what point is there in continuing our charade?

"I could call on her this afternoon," I find myself saying. "Perhaps a ride through Hyde Park?"

Father's face brightens. "An excellent suggestion. Though…" He glances out the window where dark clouds gather ominously. "The weather appears to be turning again. Mind the rain."

"A little rain never hurt anyone," I reply, already planning my afternoon. I would need to send a note ahead, of course. After last night's display, I can hardly appear unannounced at her door.

"Indeed." Father returns to his paper, but not before I catch the ghost of a smile playing at his lips. "Though perhaps pack a spare cravat. Wouldn't want to sully the family name by appearing disheveled in public."

CHAPTER TWELVE

The gentle teasing – so foreign from my usually stern father – catches me off guard. I find myself smiling despite the gravity of our previous conversation.

"And William?" He doesn't look up from his paper. "Try not to manhandle any more young ladies in public, regardless of how provoking they may be."

I feel heat creep up my neck. "Yes, sir."

"Even if they are flirting shamelessly with notorious rakes."

"Father—"

"Or batting their eyelashes at every eligible bachelor in London."

"I believe I take your meaning."

"Good." He turns a page with deliberate casualness. "Because if you ever display such a lack of control again, I shall be forced to remind you that I was once an excellent hand with a fencing foil."

I drain my coffee, hiding my smile behind the cup. "I'll bear that in mind."

Rising from the table, I catch my reflection in the window. The man looking back seems different somehow

— less rigid, more uncertain. Perhaps Father's revelation about Mother has shaken loose something in me as well.

Next Friday. My wedding day looms like the storm clouds outside, full of both promise and peril. But first, I have an afternoon ride to arrange with my reluctant bride-to-be.

Assuming, of course, she doesn't slam the door in my face.

CHAPTER THIRTEEN
a spectacle of myself
LADY ISABEL AINSWOR

I stare at the canopy of my bed, my cheeks burning with the memory of last night's events at the Huffington's dinner party. The morning sun streams through my window, but I pull the coverlet higher, wanting to hide from the world a bit longer.

What came over me? I have never acted so... improper. The way I deliberately flirted with Mr. Crawford, practically batting my eyelashes like some simpering debutante. And William—

My stomach clenches at the thought of him standing so close to Miss Fairfax, their heads bent together in intimate conversation. Even now, the image makes my blood boil. The way she simpered and preened, touching his arm with her gloved hand. The memory alone has me gripping my sheets until my knuckles turn white.

"Good morning, my lady." Margaret's cheerful voice breaks through my brooding. She's already laying out my morning dress—the pale blue muslin with delicate embroidery along the hem.

I sit up, watching as she moves about the room with practiced efficiency. "Margaret, I fear I made quite the spectacle of myself last night."

"So I heard from Mrs. Huffington's maid." Margaret's eyes dance with barely contained mirth. "She said Lord Brampton practically declared his ownership of you in front of the entire party."

"He did not own—" I stop myself, heat flooding my face. "I may have attempted to make him jealous. With Mr. Crawford."

Margaret pauses in her task of selecting my day shoes, turning to face me with raised eyebrows. "May have?"

"Well, it worked, didn't it?" I swing my legs over the side of the bed, unable to keep still. "Though I hardly expected him to react so... dramatically. *'Isabel is mine,'*" I mimic his deep voice, then throw my hands up. "As if I were a prize horse at Tattersall's!"

CHAPTER THIRTEEN

Margaret's laughter rings through the room, clear and bright. "Oh, my lady." She wipes at her eyes. "And here I thought you wanted him to notice you."

"I wanted him to—" *What did I want?* The question catches in my throat. "I simply couldn't bear watching him fawn over Miss Fairfax a moment longer. The way she kept touching his arm, looking up at him through her lashes. As if she hadn't just murdered Mozart on that pianoforte not ten minutes before!"

Margaret's shoulders shake with suppressed laughter as she helps me into my morning dress. "And your performance afterward? Was that purely to showcase your superior musical talents?"

"I..." My cheeks flush deeper. "Perhaps I wanted to remind certain parties that some of us possess actual accomplishments beyond giggling and fluttering fans."

"And it had nothing to do with drawing Lord Brampton's attention?" Margaret's knowing smile makes me want to hide behind my hands.

"Even if it did," I lift my chin, "he spent the entire time in conversation with Miss Fairfax. I doubt he heard a single note."

"Yet somehow he ended up declaring you his in front of the entire party." Margaret secures the last button and steps back, her eyes twinkling. "How fascinating."

I sink into my vanity chair, watching in the mirror as Margaret begins arranging my hair. "Do you think I went too far? With Mr. Crawford, I mean. I only meant to... to..."

"To drive Lord Brampton mad with jealousy?" Margaret suggests innocently. "Because if so, I'd say your plan worked perfectly."

"Margaret!" But I can't help the small smile that tugs at my lips. "It wasn't a plan, exactly. More of an... improvisation."

"An improvisation that ended with his lordship looking ready to challenge Mr. Crawford to a duel on the spot." Margaret secures another pin in my hair. "Really, my lady, for someone who claims to want to avoid marriage to Lord Brampton, you certainly put considerable effort into ensuring his attention remained fixed solely on you."

I open my mouth to protest, then close it again. The truth of her words strikes uncomfortably close to home. Why did it matter so much what William thought? Why did seeing him with Miss Fairfax make me want to scream? And why, when he grabbed me in front of

CHAPTER THIRTEEN

everyone and declared me his, did my heart race with something that felt suspiciously like triumph?

A knock at the door startles both Margaret and me. One of the housemaids enters, carrying a silver tray with a single letter resting upon it.

"This just arrived for you, my lady."

My heart leaps at the familiar script—William's bold, decisive hand. I snatch the letter perhaps too eagerly, breaking the seal before the maid has even left the room.

> *Lady Isabel,*
>
> *I would be honored if you would permit me to call upon you this afternoon. The weather appears favorable for a turn about Hyde Park, should you be amenable to such an excursion.*
>
> *Your most humble servant,*
> *Lord William Brampton*

"Well?" Margaret peers over my shoulder, propriety forgotten in her curiosity. "What does his lordship have to say for himself after last night's display?"

I pass her the note, watching her eyes scan the brief message. Her face breaks into a delighted smile. "You see? He wishes to spend time with you—alone! If that isn't proof he cares beyond mere possession, I don't know what is."

"It's likely just guilt over his behavior," I say, though my fingers smooth my skirts nervously. "Or perhaps his father ordered him to make amends publicly."

Margaret sets down her hairbrush with an exasperated sigh. "My lady, the man practically growled at Mr. Crawford last night. I've never heard of such naked jealousy, even in my years of service. This is not the action of a man merely following his father's orders."

"You weren't there," I protest, though my cheeks warm at the memory. "You didn't see how attentive he was to Miss Fairfax. How he bent his head to catch her every vapid word, how he—"

"And yet the moment you began paying attention to Mr. Crawford, his lordship couldn't tear his eyes away from you." Margaret resumes arranging my hair, her knowing smile reflected in the mirror. "I may not have been there, but I've heard enough from the other servants. His lordship watched your every move, growing more agitated by the minute."

CHAPTER THIRTEEN

I bite my lip, studying my reflection. "Do you really think so?"

"I know so." Margaret secures another pin. "The question is, what will you wear for your afternoon ride?"

"I haven't even accepted yet," I remind her, but my mind is already racing through my wardrobe. The new riding habit, perhaps? The deep green one that sets off my complexion so well?

"As if you could refuse." Margaret's eyes dance with mischief. "Shall I fetch the green habit? The one that made his lordship stare so intently at Lady Worthington's garden party?"

"He did not stare," I protest weakly, but heat floods my cheeks at the memory. "He merely... glanced. Once or twice."

"If you say so, my lady." Margaret's tone suggests she believes nothing of the sort. "Though I distinctly recall him nearly walking into a rosebush while 'merely glancing' in your direction."

"Margaret!" But I can't help laughing, some of my nervousness dissipating. "Very well, the green habit. But only because it's most suitable for riding."

"Of course." Margaret curtsies with exaggerated formality, her eyes twinkling. "Nothing at all to do with how it highlights your figure or brings out the gold in your eyes."

I watch her disappear into my dressing room, my stomach fluttering with anticipation. An afternoon ride with William. Alone—well, as alone as propriety allows. After last night's very public display, will he be distant? Apologetic? Or will I see that same fierce possessiveness that made my heart race when he declared me his?

The thought sends a shiver down my spine that has nothing to do with the morning's chill. I touch the letter again, tracing his bold signature with my fingertip. Perhaps Margaret is right. Perhaps this is more than duty or guilt.

But as I rise to begin penning my acceptance, doubt creeps back in. What if this is merely another move in our elaborate game? What if he's simply playing his part, maintaining appearances after last night's scene?

CHAPTER FOURTEEN
hyde park
LADY ISABEL AINSWORTH

Through the drawing-room window, I spot William's tall figure striding up the front path of Ainsworth Manor. Something seems different about his usual confident gait - he appears almost hesitant, fidgeting with his perfectly tied cravat. How peculiar.

Margaret hurries to announce him while I smooth my pale green walking dress, determined to appear utterly unaffected by his presence after last night's spectacle.

"Lady Isabel." William bows stiffly as he enters, his golden hair catching the morning light. A faint flush colors his cheeks. "I trust you are well?"

"Perfectly well, thank you." I maintain cool composure while studying his unusual demeanor. The normally eloquent Lord Brampton seems to be struggling to find words.

"I thought perhaps..." He clears his throat. "That is, would you care to take a turn about Hyde Park? The weather appears favorable for a drive."

"How thoughtful of you to suggest it." I ring for my pelisse and bonnet, noting how his fingers drum against his thigh - a nervous gesture I've never observed in him before.

William assists me into his open carriage with careful precision, though his touch through my gloves sends an unwelcome shiver down my spine. I position myself as far from him as propriety allows.

The horses set off at a leisurely pace toward Hyde Park, where the fashionable set will be out in full force to see and be seen along Rotten Row. William maintains rigid posture beside me, staring straight ahead.

The gentle sway of the carriage does nothing to distract me from William's overwhelming presence beside me. His scent - that intoxicating blend of sandalwood and leather - fills my senses with each breath. My fingers twist in my lap as I fight the urge to lean closer, to breathe him in more deeply.

CHAPTER FOURTEEN

"The weather has held rather nicely today," I prattle, desperate to fill the charged silence between us. "Though I noticed some clouds gathering to the west. Perhaps we should have brought parasols."

"Indeed." His clipped response only heightens my awareness of him.

I cannot stop my mind from wandering to our kiss in the carriage - the way his lips claimed mine with such passion, how his strong hands pulled me close. Now those same hands grip the reins with white-knuckled control, and I long to feel them on my skin again.

"The gardens are particularly lovely this time of year," I continue mindlessly, watching a pair of sparrows flit between the trees. "Mrs. Huffington mentioned her roses are already beginning to bloom."

William shifts slightly beside me, his thigh brushing against mine through our layers of clothing. The brief contact sends sparks racing through my body. I bite my lip and turn to study the passing scenery with far more attention than it deserves.

"The gardeners at Brampton Hall have been working diligently on the new conservatory," I babble on, my voice higher than usual. "Though I imagine it cannot compare to the magnificent greenhouse at Chatsworth.

Have you visited recently? I heard the Duke has acquired some remarkable specimens from—"

"Isabel." The way he says my name makes my breath catch.

"Yes?" I manage to squeak out, still determinedly avoiding his gaze.

"You're talking about conservatories."

"Well, yes. They are... quite interesting, don't you think? All that glass and... and greenery."

A small laugh escapes him - the sound makes my heart flutter traitorously in my chest. "Since when have you developed such a passionate interest in greenhouse architecture?"

"I find I have many interests you know nothing about, my lord," I reply primly, though my cheeks burn. "For instance, I am quite fascinated by... by..."

"By?" His voice holds a note of amusement that both irritates and thrills me.

"By meteorological phenomena," I finish desperately, gesturing at the sky. "Look how those clouds are forming. Most unusual patterns for this time of year."

CHAPTER FOURTEEN

"Is that so?" The warmth in his tone makes me risk a glance at his profile. The sight of his half-smile sends my stomach into a series of completely improper acrobatics.

"Absolutely." I smooth my skirts unnecessarily. "And the migration patterns of birds are equally compelling. Did you know that swallows—"

"Isabel."

"Yes?" I squeak again, cursing my betraying voice.

"You're doing it again."

"Doing what, precisely?"

"Talking about anything and everything except what's truly on your mind."

My heart pounds so loudly I'm certain he must hear it. "I'm sure I don't know what you mean. I simply believe that educated discourse on natural phenomena is both stimulating and—"

"Look at me."

I cannot resist the gentle command in his voice. When I turn, his sapphire eyes capture mine with an intensity that steals my breath. All my carefully constructed defenses crumble under that gaze.

"I..." The words die in my throat as I watch his eyes drop to my lips.

The carriage jolts over a rough patch in the road, sending me sliding closer to him. His arm instinctively steadies me, his touch burning through the fabric of my dress. We remain frozen in that position, barely breathing, painfully aware of every point where our bodies connect.

Through my peripheral vision, I spot Lady Jersey's distinctive yellow-plumed bonnet bobbing along Rotten Row, her shrewd gaze fixed upon our carriage like a hawk eyeing its prey. The Countess of Marlbury and her three daughters have also paused their morning constitutional to observe us with poorly concealed interest, no doubt already composing the letters they'll dispatch to their extensive network of gossips. Even the vendors hawking their wares seem to have developed a sudden fascination with our passage.

William's hand remains steady at my waist - propriety demands he maintain his grip lest I tumble from the carriage, yet the heat of his touch burns through my layers of muslin and cotton like a brand. I force myself to sit straighter, though the movement only serves to press me more firmly against his solid frame.

CHAPTER FOURTEEN

The whispers follow us like autumn leaves in a breeze, and I know by nightfall, every drawing room in London will be buzzing with fresh speculation about the scandalous scene at the Huffington's dinner party and its aftermath. William's jaw tightens - he too must feel the weight of society's eyes upon us, measuring and judging our every breath, our slightest interaction.

"I trust you found Mrs. Huffington's dinner entertaining last evening?" I break the tense silence with pointed sweetness.

"Quite." His jaw tightens. "Though some guests seemed determined to make spectacles of themselves."

He releases his hand on me. "Indeed. Miss Fairfax's attempts at the pianoforte were rather painful to endure."

"I was referring to certain ladies who felt compelled to throw themselves at every eligible gentleman in attendance."

My cheeks burn now. "Better than hovering around insipid debutantes like a moth to flame."

"At least Miss Fairfax knows how to conduct herself with proper decorum, unlike some who resort to shameless flirtation."

"Shameless?" I nearly choke on my outrage. "You dare accuse me of impropriety when you spent the entire evening making eyes at that simpering ninny?"

"Making eyes?" William's voice rises. "I was merely being polite, unlike your disgraceful display with Crawford!"

"Oh, so I'm not permitted to converse with other gentlemen now? Has your claim of ownership already taken effect?"

"That is not what I—" He cuts himself off, knuckles white on the reins. "You deliberately sought his attention to provoke me."

"And why should that provoke you, my lord? Unless..." I pause, studying his tense profile. "Unless you were jealous?"

William's shoulders stiffen further, if possible. "Jealous? Of that pompous puppy Crawford? Don't be absurd."

"Then why did you announce to all of London that I was 'yours'?" The memory still makes my pulse race. "Why did it matter who I spoke with?"

"Because you were trying to make *me* jealous!" He snaps, then immediately looks horrified at his own admission.

"So you admit you were jealous!" I cry triumphantly.

CHAPTER FOURTEEN

"Only because you were clearly attempting to inspire jealousy by fawning over that fool!"

A deafening crack of thunder splits the air, and suddenly the heavens unleash their fury. Fat raindrops pelt down in sheets, instantly soaking through my bonnet and pelisse. All around us, ladies shriek and gentlemen curse as the fashionable crowd scatters like startled pigeons, desperately seeking shelter.

"Hold on!" William calls over the downpour, expertly steering our carriage beneath a massive oak tree. The branches provide some protection, but water still streams through the leaves.

Without warning, William's strong hands encircle my waist. "We need better cover!" He lifts me from the carriage as if I weigh nothing, setting me gently on my feet before securing the horses.

We dash together beneath the tree's thick canopy, though it's rather too late to preserve any semblance of dignity. My carefully arranged curls are plastered to my face and neck, my muslin dress clings indecently to every curve. I attempt to wring out my skirts, very aware of William's presence mere inches away.

When I dare to look up, my breath catches. William runs his fingers through his wet hair, slicking it back from his face. Water droplets trail down his strong jaw, and his white shirt has become nearly transparent, outlining every muscled plane of his chest. His eyes meet mine, darkening with an intensity that makes my pulse race.

I step closer, drawn by some magnetic force I cannot resist. My hands rise of their own accord to rest against his chest, feeling his heart thundering beneath my palms. His breathing grows ragged.

"Isabel..." he whispers.

Then his control snaps. William's arms wrap around me, crushing me against him as his mouth claims mine with desperate passion. I melt into him, threading my fingers through his wet hair as he deepens the kiss. The rain continues to pour, but I barely notice, lost in the heat of his embrace.

Too soon, William tears his lips from mine, though he keeps me pressed close. His breath fans hot against my ear as he whispers words that stop my heart: "I love you, Isabel. God help me, I've fallen completely in love with you."

Joy bubbles up inside me, threatening to overflow. I pull back just enough to see his face, to trace my fingers along his beloved features. Droplets of water cling to his

CHAPTER FOURTEEN

eyelashes as he gazes down at me with such tender devotion it brings tears to my eyes.

I stretch up on my toes to press a soft kiss to his lips. "I cannot wait to marry you, William," I whisper against his mouth, feeling his smile.

The rain continues to fall around us, but we remain wrapped in each other's arms, sheltered in our own private paradise beneath the oak tree. For this perfect moment, the rest of the world ceases to exist - there is only William, only this overwhelming love that has captured us both so completely.

epilogue

I stand across from William, my new husband, the flickering candlelight casting shadows across his chiseled features. The wedding band on my finger still feels foreign, though not unwelcome. My heart thunders against my ribs as I take in his tall form, barely concealed by his own thin nightshirt.

"I never thought we would be here," I whisper, my voice trembling slightly. "Not after that first meeting when we plotted to appear so unsuitable for one another."

William's blue eyes darken as he takes a step toward me, and I find myself mirroring his movement. "You were never unsuitable, Isabel. Even when you were trying your hardest to appear so."

The space between us crackles with tension. I can smell his familiar scent of sandalwood and leather, mixed with something uniquely him that makes my breath catch. My fingers play with the ribbon at my throat, and I notice his gaze following the movement.

"I was rather awful to you at times," I admit, remembering our heated exchanges at various social functions. "Particularly at the Huffington's dinner party."

"As was I." His voice has dropped lower, sending shivers down my spine. "The sight of you with Crawford nearly drove me mad with jealousy."

"And you with Miss Fairfax," I counter, surprised by the lingering note of possessiveness in my voice. "I wanted to scratch her eyes out every time she simpered in your direction."

William's laugh is rich and deep. "My brilliant, passionate wife." He reaches for my hand, his thumb caressing my wedding band. "Do you know when I first realized I was falling in love with you?"

I shake my head, transfixed by the gentle motion of his thumb against my skin.

"That day in the carriage, during the storm. You were so

fierce, so alive with your anger and jealousy. I wanted nothing more than to kiss you senseless."

"You did kiss me senseless," I remind him, heat rising to my cheeks at the memory.

"Indeed." His free hand comes up to cup my face, thumb brushing across my bottom lip. "And now I can kiss you whenever I please."

My breath hitches as he leans closer, but doesn't close the final distance between us. "William," I whisper, my hands coming up to rest against his chest. Through the thin material of his nightshirt, I can feel his heart racing as fast as my own.

"Yes, my love?"

"I believe you're torturing us both with this slow approach."

His eyes spark with amusement and desire. "Perhaps I'm savoring the moment. After all, we have a lifetime of moments ahead of us."

"A lifetime of moments," I echo, sliding my hands up to his shoulders. "Starting with this one."

The tension between us builds until I can hardly breathe. William's hands settle at my waist, warm through the muslin of my shift. "Isabel," he murmurs, his voice rough with emotion, "my beautiful, maddening, perfect wife."

"Less talking," I manage to say, rising on my tiptoes. "More kissing."

His laugh turns into a groan as I press myself against him, the thin barriers of our nightclothes doing little to disguise the heat between us. "As my lady wife commands."

Our lips meet in a kiss that starts gently but quickly blazes into something more intense. William's hands tighten on my waist as mine thread through his hair, and I marvel at being able to touch him so freely. No more stolen moments in carriages or gardens. No more pretending to hate each other when every fiber of my being yearned for his touch.

As our lips part, I'm breathless and dizzy with desire. William's eyes are dark and intense, and I can see the hunger in them. He discards his nightshirt over his head, revealing his muscular chest to my wonderment.

"Don't be afraid of my body, Isabel," he whispers, reaching out to cup my face in his hands. "I want you to touch me."

EPILOGUE

I hesitate for a moment, my heart pounding in my chest. But then I nod, determined to put aside any lingering doubts or fears. I reach out and place my hand on his chest, feeling the warmth of his skin beneath my fingertips. He shudders slightly at my touch, and I can feel the rapid beat of his heart against my palm.

Emboldened by this reaction, I slide my hand down his stomach, trailing it over the muscles that ripple beneath the surface of his skin. My eyes follow the path of my hand until they rest on the erect penis that juts out from between his legs. It's a sight that both startles and excites me - a testament to the passion that burns between us.

I look up at William, who is watching me with a mixture of anticipation and lust in his eyes. Without thinking twice, I reach out and wrap my fingers around him, feeling him twitch in response to my touch. It's an intimate act - one that makes me feel both powerful and vulnerable at the same time. But as I stroke him gently, I can feel a primal urge stirring within me - an urge to claim him as mine in every possible way.

With a fierce determination, I pull William close and kiss him passionately - our tongues dancing together in a frenzied duet of desire. As we kiss, I take his hands and guide them over my body - showing him where I want him to touch me. His fingers trail over every curve and contour of my form - sending shivers of pleasure coursing through me with each caress.

William's hands roam over my waist, his touch sending shivers down my spine. He reaches up to cup my breasts through the thin fabric of my nightgown, his thumbs brushing against my nipples. I gasp at the sensation, arching into his touch. His lips trail up my neck, leaving a trail of fire in their wake. His breath fanning across my skin sends tingles down to my core.

"You taste like wine," he murmurs against my ear, his voice rough with desire.

I close my eyes, savoring the feeling of his lips on my neck. "It's the only way I could calm my nerves before our wedding night."

His tongue darts out to trace the curve of my earlobe, and I gasp softly. "You have no idea how long I've waited for this moment," he whispers, his voice thick with emotion.

I feel him move back slightly, and then his warm lips are on mine again - this time more demanding than before. His tongue explores every inch of my mouth, dancing with mine in a wild duet of passion. My body trembles with anticipation as he pulls away slightly to nip at my bottom lip.

EPILOGUE

"William," I moan, unable to form coherent thoughts as he continues to tease me with his kisses and caresses. His hands move up to undo the laces at the back of my nightgown, revealing more of my skin to his touch. I shiver at the sensation as he runs his fingers along the bare skin of my spine and over the swell of my breasts once again.

As he cups one breast in his hand, his thumb circling around the hardened nipple, I gasp into his mouth. Our kiss deepens, becoming more urgent as we explore each other's bodies for the first time since our wedding vows. My fingers twist in his hair as he pulls away from our kiss to suckle on one nipple through the thin fabric of my nightgown. The sensation is intense - both pleasurable and painful at the same time - and I can feel myself growing wet between my legs in anticipation of what's to come next.

He breaks away from me for a moment to slide down onto one knee and kisses a trail down towards where we are joined together beneath our nightclothes - his hands deftly removing what remains between us until we are both naked under each other's gaze.

He positions himself between my legs and I feel the pain first - then the fullness - as he pushes inside me. I gasp, my hands gripping his shoulders tightly. It's not unbearable, but it's certainly intense. William looks down at me with concern in his eyes, but I shake my head reassuringly.

"It's okay," I whisper, trying to sound more confident than I feel. "Just...go slow."

He nods and begins to move inside me, his eyes never leaving mine. It feels strange at first - foreign yet familiar all at once. Our bodies are learning each other's rhythms, finding a new dance together. As he pushes deeper, I bite my lip to stifle a moan, feeling every inch of him inside me. He watches me closely, his face etched with concentration and desire.

The pain subsides quickly, replaced by a growing ache that I welcome with open arms. William's movements become more confident as he starts to pick up speed, his body sliding against mine in perfect harmony. The friction is exquisite - almost too much to bear - but I don't want him to stop. My breath comes in short gasps as we move together, lost in the moment.

I cling to him tighter, arching my back slightly as he hits a particularly sensitive spot inside me. He groans softly against my neck and picks up the pace even more, his hips pumping harder against mine. The sensation is overwhelming - electrifying - and all I can do is hold on for dear life as we race towards something incredible together.

And then it hits me - like a wave crashing over me - an explosion of pleasure that takes my breath away. My body convulses around him as I cry out his name - **William!** - feeling the most wonderful sensation spread through every fiber of my being. He pauses for a moment before pulling out slowly and collapsing next to me on the bed, pulling me into his arms protectively.

"My love," he whispers against my hair, his heart racing against my earlobe just as fast as mine did during our lovemaking. "My beautiful Isabel."

I wrap my arms around him tightly, reveling in the feeling of being held by him after our passionate union. We lie there for what feels like hours, our hearts beating in sync under the thin sheet that covers us both now post-coitus blissfully sleepy and contented until exhaustion takes over completely...

I drift into a peaceful slumber, William's strong arms wrapped around me, his steady breathing a lullaby against my neck. As sleep claims me, my mind wanders into the sweetest of dreams.

In my dream, I sit in the nursery at Brampton House, sunlight streaming through tall windows onto a beautifully carved cradle. The room smells of lavender and fresh linens, and a gentle breeze carries the scent of roses from the garden below. In my arms, I hold the most precious bundle I've ever seen - our son.

He's perfect in every way, with William's golden hair and striking blue eyes. His tiny fingers wrap around my index finger with surprising strength as he gazes up at me with complete trust and adoration. His cherubic face holds all of his father's handsome features in miniature - the same strong jawline, the same aristocratic nose, even the same slight dimple in his left cheek when he smiles.

"My darling boy," I whisper, running a finger along his soft cheek. He responds with a coo that melts my heart, his little mouth forming a perfect 'O' as he yawns. The weight of him in my arms feels right, natural, as if this is what I was always meant to do.

I begin humming a lullaby, one my own mother used to sing to me, and rock gently in the chair. The baby's eyes start to drift closed, but he fights sleep like his father does, determined to stay awake just a moment longer. His tiny hand still grips my finger, and I marvel at how something so small can hold my heart so completely.

The nursery around us is a perfect blend of both William and me - his family's traditional furniture mixed with the artistic touches I've added. A mobile of delicate paper birds hangs above the cradle, turning slowly in the breeze. On the walls, I've painted scenes from our favorite fairy tales, the ones we'll read to him as he grows.

"You're going to be just like your papa," I tell him softly, touching his little nose. "Strong and brave and kind. But please, darling, don't inherit his stubborn streak. One of those in the family is quite enough."

The baby makes a sound that could almost be a laugh, and my heart swells with love. His eyes, so like William's, focus on my face with an intensity that takes my breath away. I can see both of us in him - my curiosity, William's determination, our shared passion for life.

I rise from the rocking chair, careful not to disturb him as he finally surrenders to sleep. Walking to the window, I show him the grounds of what will one day be his inheritance. "This will all be yours someday, my love," I whisper. "But more importantly, you'll always have our love. That's the greatest inheritance of all."

The baby sighs contentedly in his sleep, his perfect little face peaceful and serene. I press a gentle kiss to his forehead, breathing in that indescribable scent that only babies have. My heart feels so full it might burst with love for this tiny person who represents everything William and I share.

"I love you, my precious boy," I murmur against his soft hair. "More than all the stars in the sky… more than all the music in the world."

THE END

you might also like

marquess made for me
DOLLAR PRINCESS SERIES - BOOK 3

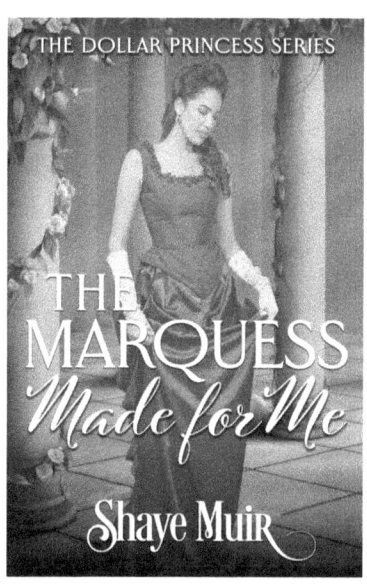

UNRAVEL A LOVE STORY WOVEN ACROSS CONTINENTS

In the bustling heart of 1870s New York, a captivating tale unfolds...

Victoria Giordano, the jewel of a wealthy Italian immigrant family, prepares for a grand proposition. Her ambitious father seeks not just a husband, but a Marquess from across the Atlantic!

Enter the Marquess of Wynehill, a man of exquisite taste and dwindling fortune. Desperate to maintain his extravagant lifestyle, he turns his sights westward - to the land of opportunity, America!

Will their union be a masterpiece, a love story woven from desire and destiny? Or will their contrasting backgrounds unravel their carefully stitched romance?

Dive into "The Marquess Made for Me," a dazzling historical romance where old-world charm meets American ambition.

Pre-order your copy today and be swept away by a love story as rich as the garments they treasure!

Dollar Princess Series - Book 3

Ebook & Paperback

love in winter

LOVE LOST IN THE SEASON? SEARCHING FOR A WARM EMBRACE

Is Lady Alicia destined for a loveless marriage or a life on the shelf?

Follow Lady Alicia Henley's plight as societal pressures force her into the London Season. At twenty-five, she's adept at dodging suitors and yearns for something more than a preordained match.

But as the season closes and options dwindle, a drastic choice presents itself.

Will she settle for a loveless union or embark on a daring adventure across the sea?

The Caribbean beckons with the promise of sunshine and perhaps love.

Dive into a captivating tale of defying expectations and finding love in the most unexpected places.

Love in Winter is perfect for readers who adore:

- Regency Romance with a Twist
- Strong Female Leads Who Break the Mold
- Exotic Adventures that Heat Up the Pages

Escape the Ballroom and Discover Where True Love Waits!

A Regency Standalone Novella

Ebook & Paperback

love without warning

WHEN LOVE IS FOUND UNEXPECTEDLY

Miss Lydia Browning was the daughter of a wealthy tea merchant. Contracted to marry The Earl of Harwick when she was ten, Lydia tried everything to get out of the arranged marriage to the Gentry she found old and boring.

The Earl bought Lydia for a bargain price; now, her dowry was five times greater than when the contract was first reached. All would be grand if Lydia did not despise Lord Harwick, so how was the Gentleman supposed to strike up a conversation when all Lydia did was scowl and run away?

A Regency Standalone Novella

Available in

Ebook & Paperback

about shaye

Shaye Muir is an emerging author of Historical Romance. Mrs. Muir has many writing interests and lives an incognito digital lifestyle.

Mrs. Muir is part of the Ardent Artist Books family and loves to write Regency and Romance Series.

Mrs. Muir has published several books.

also by shaye

DOLLAR•PRINCESS•SERIES

The Penny Bride - Book 1

The Misguided Bride - Book 2

The Marquess Made For Me - Book 3

STANDALONES

Love Without Warning

Love in Winter

The Earl's Impossible Bargain

The Maritime Deception

www.ingramcontent.com/pod-product-compliance
Lightning Source LLC
LaVergne TN
LVHW010205070526
838199LV00062B/4510